Broadcast Wasteland

Ben Van Dongen

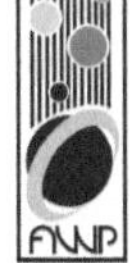

For my Grandparents
Who would say how
wonderful it is no matter what
they thought.

Broadcast Wasteland

The Synthetic Albatross Series
Book Three

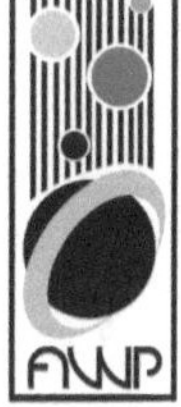

One
The Moons and the Clouds

A cool wind raced up the communications tower and through the grated platform near the top, ruffling Luc's dark hair. He was on his back, watching the random openings in the dense cloud cover, spotting pieces of the large blue moon and the smaller, yellowish rocks that orbited it. Rolling onto his side, he traced the cable connecting the tower's terminal to his pocket computer. The small device was open, the flip-top screen displaying the download progress. Dings and scratches covered the surface and stickers concealed more. Periodic whirs and clicks emanated from the micro-disc port.

"Seventy-two percent," he said and leaned back again.

A voice came over his headphones. He had one speaker slipped off to the side. "Is that good? Is that bad? You've got to give me some reference here."

"Just mumbling to myself, Anna." Luc closed his eyes and felt the dull, pocked metal of the platform, cool against his hand.

"I wish you'd fill me in more. I'm supposed to be learning from you, but I'm down here keeping watch, in the dark. I can hear things moving. It's not safe to be alone outside the city."

"You're not alone."

"I feel alone. And I think there are some wild dogs sniffing around."

"Anna, I'm right here." Luc sat up with a grunt and looked through the platform. The bottom of the tower was dark. Small, empty shacks and hovels made of scavenged materials were clustered around the base, like fungus growing at the foot of a massive tree. The tenants had been forcibly evicted by security days earlier. Some of the cables used to tap power from the communications tower were still hanging between the homes. Luc thought of massive snakes.

"You're fifty metres away."

"Closer to a hundred." He yawned and checked his watch. Touching a button on the side illuminated the face unevenly. In the centre of the circular display, behind the analogue dials, was a small, rectangular screen showing a miniature progress bar for the download. "Look, it's nearly one in the morning, the download is at eighty percent. How about we finish up here, rush to the diner, and make the copies over some breakfast?

"That sounds nice, but it doesn't do anything about these dogs."

Luc laughed and lay back down. "If they get too close, shine a light in their face and kick the nearest can. That should scare them off."

"Can you remind me again why we have to keep hacking into the towers in order to listen to the broadcast?"

Getting to his feet, Luc picked up his computer. It was about the width and length of his hand and just about twice as thick with the screen closed. Holding it in both hands, he used his thumbs to type in a line of code. "They piggyback their signal on the local Consortium broadcast, but they scramble it differently every time. We need to get access to what the government is sending in order to separate the two."

"Then we decode the signal?"

"Then I decode the signal with the scripts I've written and distribute it." Luc checked the download. The progress bar was at eighty-seven percent.

"Okay," Anna said. "I get that, but why are we always the ones who hack the towers?"

Luc shrugged, realized he was alone on the platform, and frowned. "Someone has to. Besides, I look forward to the broadcast. I don't need some desk jockey botching the whole thing and end up missing it for a week."

"We could always pick up a bootleg from Helmut."

Luc swung his fist, imagining the skinny, pimply-faced young man. "I'm not paying that joker for nothing. The quality is shit and the price he charges is outrageous."

"I'm just saying. It's dangerous to keep sneaking out of the city every week, especially with corporate security rounding everyone up and tearing the place down. Someone else can take some of the slack, can't they?"

"What do you think you're doing here?" Luc looked through the grate again and saw a sliver of light sweeping back and forth. "And don't forget, you're supposed to be keeping watch for patrols."

"I am," Anna said. "I'm watching for dogs, too."

The light pointed up at Luc. The beam had no chance of reaching him, but he moved closer to the centre structure anyway. "There aren't any dogs. That light is going to attract unwanted attention."

"You told me to shine the light."

"In the faces of dogs. Again, there are no dogs." Luc leaned against the bulk of the tower. The metal hummed slightly. A gust of wind whistled through the metal grate. He pulled up the hood on his sweatshirt. "Eighty-nine percent."

The light went out. "It's cold."

"You think it's cold down there?" Luc tapped his foot against the tower.

"It's not a competition. I'm not suddenly warm because it happens to be colder at the top of the tower than on the ground. My complaint is valid."

"Fine." Another stiff breeze made Luc's sweatshirt billow. He closed his eyes and imagined himself falling off the edge of the tower, taking just over a second to hit the ground. A sensation of vertigo overcame him and he took a wide step to stop from falling over. He huffed and felt his pulse race.

"Luc?"

"Yeah?"

"How much time is left?"

Checking the display, Luc heard the tiny disc spinning in the tiny computer. The progress bar was most of the way across the screen. "Ninety-two."

"Oh, that's a good jump. I think. Is it?"

"I guess. It's going more slowly than normal, like there's something interfering with the signal." Luc looked up, imagining the satellites circling the planet and what might be messing with them.

"What could be causing that?"

Luc shrugged. "Who knows. Maybe there's some ship up there from another corporation hacking into the network."

"Really?" Anna's voice pitched up with excitement.

Luc chuckled. "Just a joke. No one cares about this rock. As soon as this thing is done downloading I'll climb down and we can get out of here."

"That's the worst part."

Luc sat cross-legged on the deck and stared out at the distant city. The wall encircling it, twenty feet high around the whole perimeter, had lights set at regular intervals shining into the waste. The buildings behind it seemed to sit on top, making them look like they rose from a single massive structure. It was as if the city was a huge flying saucer, ready to take flight. "Good riddance."

"What?"

"Nothing." Luc shook his head. "What's the worst part?"

"Waiting for you to climb down. It takes forever and I'm convinced that you'll fall."

"I haven't fallen yet."

"That's not reassuring."

"I wasn't trying to be." The clouds moved in front of the bulk of the main moon, darkening the night. Looking out over the waste, Luc spotted something moving in between the tower and the city. A set of lights flew from spot to spot, hovering above sections of the shantytown. They searched one area, moved to another then repeat the process—and they were headed towards them. "Anna?"

"What?" Her tone was flat.

"You see those shuttles?" Luc stood.

"What? Where?" The light came on again.

"Turn that off!" Following the cable from his computer to the port he had broken into on the tower, Luc prepared to yank it. "They're sweeping this way. Coming from the north-west. Start heading back now. Take the long way around."

"What about you?" The light went off.

"I'm at," Luc checked the screen, "ninety-six percent. As soon as it's done, I'll pull the plug and follow. Make sure to keep an eye out for ground patrols."

"Just leave the download, Luc. It's not worth getting caught."

"I'm close, ninety-seven. It'll take me time to get down anyway." Wrapping up the loose cable, Luc tapped his foot. "What were you doing out here after curfew?"

"I was out scavenging and lost track of the time. There was a pack of dogs that had me pinned in a shack. The one with the flowers painted all over it. I had to kill one of them to get away."

"Good." Luc glanced down. "But too specific. They'll check for remains."

"I saw some on the way here."

"Great. Good. Go!"

"But—"

"Ninety-eight. Just go, already." Luc pulled his headphones off and watched the patrol stop at another, seemingly random spot, their lights scanning the ground below. "Come on." The hum from the disc picked up speed and the progress bar crept towards the edge of the screen.

The lights moved closer and started to scan the nearest radio tower. The ships split, one going under the thick cables running between the towers, the other going over. They finished searching to the base and turned towards Luc.

The download ended with an audible ping from the headphones and a green blink on the small screen. Luc pulled the cord free from the tower, snapped his computer shut, and stuffed them both into an inner jacket pocket. Leaving the panel lying on the platform, he ran for the ladder and started to climb down.

Two
Through What Remains

The searchlights illuminated the top spire of the tower, the beams from the two ships playing cat and mouse, chasing each other over the structure. Luc climbed down the ladder as quickly as he could, alternating his focus from the approaching shuttles to his grip on the rungs. The lights reached the platform and held their position.

"Shit." Grimacing, Luc realized that he hadn't replaced the cover over the access port. Putting his hands and feet on the outside of the ladder, he let himself slide. He reached a mounting point, climbed around it, and continued his rapid descent. The ships finished searching the top of the tower and started to spiral down around the structure. They moved in unison on opposite sides, their beams of light like a physical tether. Luc reached a small landing and swung himself around the ladder. Hugging the widening spire, he shuffled to the far side, trying to avoid the lights.

He looked for a gap in the beams, but the paths of the shuttles were precise. Finding an alcove in the wall where one tower section locked into the next, he stood facing the corner. "Did the Consortium just happen to put their best pilots on tonight's shift?"

One of the spotlights scanned past him, stopped, and moved back. "Attention, citizen." The voice of the pilot boomed from loudspeakers on the outside of the ship. "You are currently in violation of the following statutes. Decree seven-eight-two, out of city limits after curfew, twelve-sixty-one, found in restricted area, five-nine-four, unauthorized proximity to corporate structures, including official buildings, radio towers, warehouses, and spaceports. You are also suspected of tampering with this tower. Stay where you are and prepare to be taken into custody. Consortium patrols are inbound." The second beam joined the first and Luc squinted at the reflection of them off the tower.

Making sure his hood was up, he shuffled towards the ladder, keeping his back to the pilots.

"Remain where you are. Officers will apprehend you on site."

"No thanks." Walking backwards, Luc reached behind him to grab the ladder. As soon as his hand was on it, a dart struck the tower next to him. It flashed blue as arcs of electricity burst from it and into the metal wall. In a single motion, Luc gripped the rail, swung himself to the outside, and slid down the ladder as quickly as he dared. His hands just skimmed the surface creating friction burns on his palms.

"Citizen, halt!" Several more shots rang out, piercing over the thrum of the ships. Another dart ricocheted off of a rung where Luc's hand had been.

The ladder ended at the next platform and Luc squeezed his feet against the rails, smelling burning rubber from the souls of his shoes. He grabbed a rung, jolting himself to a stop short of the bottom and leapt off the ladder, avoiding a well-aimed dart. Landing with a clatter, he used momentum to steady himself and ran for the door to the interior stairwell.

The shuttles followed him, their spotlights locked onto his movements. "Stop where you are, you can't escape."

At the doorway, Luc dropped into a slide, scooping up a rock he had used to prop open the metal door. It slammed shut behind him as more darts rained against it, their electric charge buzzing across the surface.

The inside of the radio tower was dimly illuminated by emergency lights. A staircase hugged the outer wall enclosed between it and an interior one where cables and electronic components ran up the centre of the structure. Luc raced down the steps, passing periodic landings leading to small doorways that opened farther into the tower.

Another proclamation from one of the pilots echoed off the metal walls, distorting into gibberish by the time it met Luc near the ground. Out of breath, he stopped at the bottom door.

"Okay. Troops on the way, two ships watching for me." Holding his side, Luc huffed, visualizing his route out of the radio tower. "I've got to cross the fenced-in lot, avoid those shuttles all the way to the checkpoint, and steer clear of the soldiers." He checked his watch. The hands glowed a dim, phosphorescent green over top of the dark display. It was twenty after one. "Forty minutes. I can do that."

Shaking out his hands, Luc prepared for the sprint to the nearest shacks, hoping to lose the searchlights quickly. With a shake of his head, he hip checked the crash bar and ran for the hole in the fence. As he crouched, sharp pain shot through his knee and he grimaced, ignoring it.

The lights from the ships were separately scanning the base of the tower. Luc watched the path of the nearest one as it arced in front of him. He slid to a stop and spun away as it swept right through his path. He murmured a thanks to nothing in particular as he ran to the fence and ducked through the hole he'd cut on his way in. The second light followed a wider circle and he had to scramble back to his feet and sprint for the closest building.

The shacks around the tower were made from scrap collected by the former residents. Odd pieces of fibreboard, rusty corrugated metal, plastic panels, worn tops of tables, and a hundred other random items were fastened together in as many ways. Each one was just large enough for a couple people to store some scrounged things and squeeze into to get out of the rain or shelter against the cold winters. An odd maze of streets had developed between the dense clusters of hovels, most just wide enough for some pedestrian traffic. A few, wider like boulevards, had a market grow in the open spaces around them. Luc didn't know the entire labyrinth by heart, but he had spent time in the market and had memorized his routes to the towers.

He made it to the first building and squeezed in between it and its neighbour before the light could catch him. It whipped past quickly, frantically searching. Using one of the wooden walls, he pulled himself free and ran down the curving street, kicking up puffs of dirt. The path came to a dead end, but Luc climbed over one of the huts, using a discarded barrel and a makeshift windowsill. He jumped from that roof to another and dropped down the other side onto the boulevard. Looking back at the tower, he saw the ships moving away from it, widening their search.

A few heavy drops hit the dirt next to him before a downpour of rain erupted from the sky. He felt a rumble in his feet but didn't notice a corresponding flash of lightning. Shrugging his shoulders against the cold water, he jogged towards the city wall and the nearest checkpoint. Farther ahead, he spotted a cluster of smaller lights sweeping the street and the shacks on either side.

"Shit. Search party already?" Luc found the nearest alley between the stalls and headed into the abandoned market.

Three
Black Market

The market, a twisting series of corridors, ran behind the larger and better-constructed buildings first put up outside the city. Luc remembered that, for a while, the shantytown was considered a natural extension, like the villages that clustered around castles. But as it grew, it became less structured. The desperation of the people was reflected in the small, crammed-together shacks that had deteriorated into slums. The market turned black as crime became rampant. It was the underground nature that had drawn Luc in the first place. As he passed abandoned stalls, he remembered the used computer components and banned programs he had bought from the sly and suspicious vendors.

Most of the market was covered by a makeshift roof that protected it from the elements and added a sense of concealment from the Consortium ships and satellites. Luc had been there on a raid and only escaped due to the kindness of one of the regular shopkeepers he frequented. The woman had led him through a well-hidden door into one of the reputable stores facing the boulevard.

He bumped into a stall as he stumbled around in the near blackness. The tight beam of a flashlight cut through farther ahead and was quickly joined by two more. They crisscrossed as the soldiers entered the market from another alley. Luc crouched low and moved behind the nearest stall, hugging the rough wood facade. Rain pelted the roof, making as many different sounds as there were materials, drowning out the noise made by the searchers. There was a boom in the distance with another corresponding rumble through the ground.

Watching the beams play off of the stands and the wall behind him, Luc slipped from one hiding place to the next, trying to skirt around them. He managed to get to the leftmost wall that led to a small hallway going deeper into the market when one of the lights stopped moving and focused on a stall near him. The beam tightened as the security guard approached. Pointing his ear towards the officers, Luc tried to block out the pinging of the rain hitting the tin roof above him.

"—saw something over here." Luc heard a faint crunch as the man stepped on some discarded thing left after the market was evacuated. "What are our orders if we find this joker anyway?"

A higher pitched voice joined the first as another light was trained on the stall. "Have to take them in. We're not supposed to shoot them."

"What kind of crap is that? Are we just supposed to ask nicely?"

"If I find whoever got me out of the warm barracks and into this shit, I'm going to at least wing'em."

"Hey!" A third officer shouted from farther away. "Did you two find something over there or what?"

The beams turned away, haphazardly dancing along the ground.

"This new guy running things has no idea how to deal with this hacker-want-to-be scum. I say, round them all up and put them to work in the mines."

The high voiced guard snorted. "Mine what? This rock has been empty for over a year. If it weren't so close to trading routes, the Consortium would have already abandoned it."

"Where'd you hear that bullshit?"

The guards started walking away. Luc let out a breath and scuttled to the next stall.

"I overheard the commander..." the voices were lost in the sound of the rain.

Luc darted to another counter, pushing through the open corner of a tarp draped over the front. A beam zeroed in on the spot, shining through the blue plastic. He heard rushed footsteps as the soldiers shouted to each other.

"Over there!"

"Damn it. Did you walk right past him?"

Shutting his eyes tightly, Luc breathed through his teeth, hoping they would miss him again. As the second and third flashlights pointed at his location, he prepared to run.

Squinting, he spotted a slice of dim light coming in through an open section of the roof along with the rain. It was dark between him and the illuminated spot but he knew the stall that was there. Probably. If he was right, it was his chance to escape. The ground shook again, making Luc tense.

The first guard slid to a stop in front of the tarp. Luc lunged upward, hurling the counter into the man and ran.

"There!" The first light found him, showing him bits of his path blocked by his own shadow. "Halt!"

A bullet zipped past, obliterating an old wooden sign. Luc sidestepped a fallen chair and changed direction as quickly as he could. Another shot hit the nearest wall as the second beam joined the first.

"Stop shooting you morons," one of the guards yelled.

Luc crouched as he ran, trying to balance speed and cover, heading for the opening to the next section of the market. He kicked out the leg of a table and pulled down a rickety stall, obstructing the chokepoint.

The soldiers were close behind, crashing their way through the narrow aisles, their flashlights bobbing and weaving. The lights stopped at the barrier Luc had made but they fired off another volley.

Dropping to his belly, Luc winced, but managed to avoid the barrage. Crawling behind a counter, he scrambled for the stall under the open roof. He heard a loud crash and guessed the soldiers had made it through his makeshift barricade.

The three beams of light danced around the smaller area as Luc wriggled through the mud to the spot he was looking for. "Come on, be the right one."

Against the wall, behind the soaked and rotting stall, was a large metal grate made from tarnished bronze. Leaves and flowers twisted around each other on the ornate surface. "Yes." Luc sighed as he pushed a finger through the oddly shaped gaps and found the hidden clasp. The grate swung inward and he crawled through the opening, kicking it closed as soon as he was inside.

The small shaft ended in a sharp turn and a dead end. Luc knew there was some secondary secret in the tight space that the building owner and stall operator, an old woman less than half his size, used to get into the basement, but he'd never been privy to the information. Luc had used the secret tunnel as a hiding place, for a small fee, but he had never been to the other side. He tried to suck in his chest and stomach and squeeze around the corner, but quickly gave up. Instead, he waited, making as little noise as possible.

Looking past his feet, he watched through the grate. The lights came in and out of view as the soldiers searched, but, eventually, they disappeared entirely. Luc considered that they were waiting for him, turning off their lights, engineering a trap. Then he thought about the Consortium soldiers and snickered to himself. The real trouble were the Operatives. He had only seen an Operative once, during a raid. They were efficient, organized, and terrifying. One of the captured hackers had tried to run, and the hole in her body appeared like magic. Luc was appropriately afraid of the Operatives in their blacked-out helmets and state-of-the-art armour. The soldiers who worked as guards and patrols were mostly locals looking for a steady paycheck and a little power. They were mostly incompetent, lazy, and corrupt—not the type to wait in the dark and wet in case their quarry was hiding.

Still, Luc waited another ten minutes before

crawling back out of the grate. It took him another five to find the right spot to press with his foot to open it. Backing out of the tight space, he felt his heart speed up. The small section of the market seemed empty. He kept low as he closed the grate. His arms and legs ached from the confined space, but he headed deeper into the market as quickly and quietly as he could.

His hands outstretched, feeling his way as much as seeing, Luc manoeuvred his way through the maze of stalls, keeping an eye open for more flashlights.

Lightning streaked across the sky. The uncovered sections of the market were briefly as bright as day before collapsing back into night.

A loud rumble rode the tail end of the flash, making the wooden stalls tremble. The rainfall increased to a torrent, the drops striking the roof and ground with continuous thuds.

Luc managed to reach the end of the market without running into any more guards. The city wall was close, a couple hundred metres away. It loomed over the buildings that huddled in its shadow and the bright spotlights shining down from it reached even the dark market. The city skyline rose behind it in shadow, the lightning highlighting their outlines in brief flashes.

Picking an alley leading away from the direction of the checkpoint, Luc hoped to avoid any guards still looking for him. He didn't know how he would talk his way through. They would suspect him as the person who hacked into the tower, but he didn't think they could prove it was him. Either way, crouching in the shadows, he made a copy of his recording. He hid one micro-disc inside a secret pocket in the lining of his jacket and put the other in his music player, leaving an empty disc in his pocket computer.

Patting the disc in its secret compartment, he went down the alleyway and walked into an open field.

The buildings he was expecting to sneak around were gone and piles of rubble were scattered in their place. A huge bulldozer smashed into the building next to him and right into the abandoned market behind. The sound of the engine and squeaking, mashing of the treads were practically drowned out by the pelting rain but he felt the reverberation.

Luc saw more giant machines pulling, crashing, and tearing the structures down. A strip of land over a hundred metres wide was already cleared as far as he could see. Before he could run, three guards came around the bulldozer, their guns and lights trained on him. Luc put up his hands.

Four
Checkpoint

The checkpoint was a small, concrete structure built into the side of the city wall. Next to the little out-cropped building was a set of huge metal doors reserved for transports and other large vehicles. Red lights shone in the open windows of the checkpoint and spilled into the cloud-covered night, illuminating the rippling puddles collecting in the mud. Luc's hair was plastered to his head and droplets found their way inside his jacket. He fought his body's natural reaction to shiver against the cold wind, but shook anyway.

One of the guards went through the concrete doorway, taking his helmet off once inside. The others stood with Luc, stamping their feet and fidgeting.

The soldier on his left took a step towards the opening in the wall. "Hey, hurry up in there, I want to get out of the rain."

The guard inside waved dismissively while talking to a woman behind a small metal desk. After a few moments of back and forth, they were beckoned inside. Even with bare walls, the checkpoint was warmer than the rain soaked night. Luc blinked water out of his eyes and wiped his face against his shoulder, his hands still bound behind his back.

He was shoved towards the woman behind the desk and stumbled, colliding with the metal surface. A hand grabbed him by the scruff and pulled him upright.

"This is the guy you found on the radio tower?" The woman asked.

"Yeah. We chased him through the market and caught him in the deconstruction zone." Luc couldn't see who was speaking, but the man's voice was clear, so he assumed it was the guard who had taken his helmet off.

"Okay. Scan him." The woman crossed her arms and sat back. She nodded to the end of her desk.

The man holding Luc shoved his face toward the device. It was a glowing pad with multiple cross points on it, each one with hatched measurement lines through them. It was partially enclosed on the back and sides, just wider than Luc's head. He winced as his face was pressed against the glass, his eyes shut.

"Sir, look at the screen and don't blink." The woman sounded bored. She stifled a yawn and cleared her throat.

As soon as Luc opened his eyes, the scan started. A line of green light moved down as a red line went right. When it was finished the scanner let out a little beep. It was an incongruent sound—almost cute.

He was hauled upright again and faced the woman as she read the generated report. She sighed as she finished and pulled out a dirty, plastic basket from a stack behind her desk. "Put his stuff in here."

The closest soldier turned Luc to face him and started to pull things out of his jacket. He took the duplicate micro-disc he'd made easy to find, his pocket computer, music player, wallet, keys, cords and whatever he could find. He even pulled the headphones from Luc's neck and the watch from his wrist.

The woman glanced at her flickering screen, the pale amber light washing out her features. "Check the lining of his jacket."

Luc glared at her, his mouth partially open. The guard stuffed his hand inside his jacket and rustled around for the hidden pocket. His hand snagged on it and with a jerking lunge, he reached in and pulled out the micro-disc.

"What do we have here?"

"Drop it in the basket and bring him to the special director." Her gaze flicked up to one of the guards behind Luc.

"What? I'm counting on this collar to meet my quota."

The woman glowered at them, her eyes half open. "I don't make the rules. I just process the degenerates."

"Come on," the guard said.

"Take this crap. I'm not processing it." She pushed the basket. The first guard snatched it off the edge of the desk, grumbling.

They left the small room and went through an interior doorway with a large metal hatch hanging open.

Still held by the scruff, Luc was pushed into the door. He bounced off of it and followed the guard down a hallway. The corners of the hall cut in at a soft angle and red lights shone from behind them. There was a room marking the midpoint down the hallway that led to an identical entryway on the city side of the wall. Instead of going down to the end, the guard in the lead stopped at another metal door set into the concrete. He knocked against it hard, the sound reverberating on the smooth walls. A slit at eye level opened.

"I've got the detainee."

The slit closed and the door opened with a click and a slight hiss. It swung slowly inward on large hinges. The room was square with a couple of desks on either side of the doorway. Consortium security employees were typing away at the terminals and didn't look up. The soldier who had been guarding the door stood off to the side as they entered.

The guard without his helmet stopped next to him. "How'd you get a job inside tonight? We've been out in the rain after this waste-case."

"Guess I'm lucky." The soldier's voice was deep behind the helmet.

Luc was pushed farther into the room.

A woman in a suit came through a doorway on the far wall. Her hair was tied back making her expression seem severe. She was short, especially next to the large soldiers, but she walked up to them with her nose in the air, seemingly unaware of the size difference. She held a state-of-the-art tablet under her arm, but she looked up and to the side before talking to them.

Luc squinted at her, trying to see if there was any sign that she had an implant. He had only heard of the Consortium Operatives or executives having actual implants. The tablet was impressive enough. It was decades ahead of his makeshift pocket computer, but an implant would be light-years more advanced.

"There you are," the woman said. "The director has been waiting. Get this detainee into the interrogation room immediately."

"Yes, ma'am." The guards saluted, but Luc caught the scowl the helmetless officer made. He figured the man was used to having his expressions hidden behind the black visor. They headed for the doorway in the same order, the guard without his helmet, Luc, and the two other soldiers behind him. Luc caught sight of a metal chair and table in the room before the first guard blocked his view.

"Stop!" The woman stomped up to the man, her shoes clicking against the concrete floor.

"What?"

"Did I tell you to go into the interrogation room?"

The man furrowed his brow. "You said—"

"I told you to get the hacker into the interrogation room, not for you, or anyone else to go in there."

"But. Who's going to protect you?"

Her jaw clenched, she leaned toward the guard. "Why do I need protection?"

"Ma'am, it's customary for interrogators to have at least one guard present." The man straightened, avoiding her eyes.

"Who said I was the interrogator?"

"I…uh."

Taking a step back, the woman sneered. "Never mind. Get that man into the room, now."

The guard holding Luc let go. "Yes, ma'am." He gave Luc a shove, sending him through the doorway.

Stopping himself before he collided with the wall, Luc turned in time to see the door close behind him. He sighed and kicked over the chair.

"No need for that."

Luc looked up. Someone was on the other side of the table, his feet up.

Broadcast Wasteland

Five
Old Friends

"Dmitri? What the hell are you doing here?" Luc squinted at the man. He was wearing a light grey suit with the black and red Consortium patch over his breast pocket. Thin stripes of the same colours ran around the collar of his jacket and blended with his tie. His dirty blond hair hung over the side of his face and he flung it back with a flick of his head.

Standing, Dmitri smiled. "Haven't pieced it together yet?"

Luc glowered. "I knew you sold out, went to the Consortium for a job."

"And they made me Special Director in charge of Computerised Criminal Acts." Moving around the table, Dmitri patted Luc on his shoulder. He was half a head shorter, even in his dress boots. "I'm cracking down on you and your hacker buddies. Making this a cleaner, safer colony for the good citizens of TRAPPIST."

"Me? Hack? Perish the thought." Luc glanced at him out of the corner of his eye and forced an awkward smile.

"Come on, Luc. We've been friends since we were kids running around the back alleys, getting into trouble. We used to work in the same crew." Dmitri sat on the table.

"Do they know that?" Luc nodded towards the door and the Consortium employees on the other side.

With a chuckle, Dmitri tossed his hair back again. "Of course. How do you think I convinced them to put me in charge of this special operation?"

"It certainly wasn't your charm."

"Classy as always." Dmitri's smile faded. "So, why were you out for a stroll, in the middle of the night, in the outskirts, after curfew?"

Luc stared at Dmitri, unblinking. "You know me. Scrounging for scraps out in the slums. Not that there's much left after the Governor cleared it out and arrested everyone living there. Any chance you know where he took them? It wasn't on vacation, was it?"

"They were given jobs, actually."

"Let me guess." Luc sniffed. "In the mines?"

Dmitri crossed his arms. "What else is there on this rock?"

"And you're okay with them sending poor, weak people into the empty mines to dig deeper and deeper in hopes of finding anything worth as much as the equipment they're using to dig with?"

Dmitri glanced up, above Luc. "Have to do something productive. Not much else worth anything on this planet but the minerals. If we weren't so close to an interstellar crossroad, the Consortium would have abandoned us long ago."

Luc rolled his eyes. "You know, I overhead something about that. It would be such a shame."

"It would, actually." Dmitri clenched his jaw. "They're the only thing keeping us fed, keeping the power on."

"It's certainly a good thing for traitors like you."

Dmitri shot to his feet, knocking the table back. His hair cascaded over his face. "Still as petulant as ever. You never could see the bigger picture with your head up your own ass." Taking a breath, Dmitri brushed his hair back. "What was I supposed to do? Go down into the empty mines and die, like my parents? I had Anna to think of. I had to put food on the table and hacking towers, running from the soldiers, going to bed hungry. It wasn't working for me anymore. So I grew up and made the smart choice. It's not my fault you're so high on your horse that you'd rather get caught and become a martyr for those loser hackers who look up to you. What do any of you contribute? Really?"

Luc snorted. "Contribute to what? Corruption? Enslavement? Forced evacuations and work camps? Someone has to stand up to the Consortium."

Dropping his shoulders and snickering to himself, Dmitri shook his head. "You call what you do standing up? Breaking into unsecure databases, petty crimes, that radio show you worship? If the Consortium saw you as anything more than an annoying mosquito, they would rain so much horror down on you that you'd wish you were dead. You're a bug and I'm going to swat you."

"And get a pat on the head?"

"Exactly. And a place to live for my sister and me, and enough food to eat, and comfort, and stability."

Luc sneered. "And an implant."

Smiling, Dmitri bobbled back and forth slightly. "Noticed that, did you? Much nicer than that hand-held device you scrabbled together from spare parts."

"You're nothing more than a sell-out working for a monster who crushes the rest of us under its thumb." Luc sighed. "So? What're you going to do to me?"

Dmitri went to the table and moved it back into place. He righted the chair that Luc had kicked over, and sat on the other side. "Let's get down to business." He gestured for Luc to join him.

Shrugging, Luc turned to show his bound hands.

"Come on. It's not that hard."

Luc scowled and glanced at the closed door then back at Dmitri. Slowly, he sauntered to the chair and sat.

"We both know you hacked into the tower."

"You can't prove it."

Dmitri smiled again. "I don't have to. I have enough on you as it is and circumstances being as they are, I can assume it was you." He tossed his hair back. "Hell, I really don't need much of a reason anyway."

"Fine. What do you want? You didn't put together this whole special assignment just to catch me."

"Oh, it goes much deeper than you. In fact, you were little more than a blip on their radar before I came along." Dmitri leaned on the table, his smile faltering. "But I need something from you. I know you've been hanging out with my sister. That she's been learning the trade from you. It's going to stop, now. I'm not going to have her mixed up in your kind of trouble—not with the hammer I'm about to drop down on you and your old friends. Think of this as your one opportunity to escape what's coming. Get my sister to stop. Keep her away from the others and help me end this little tantrum she's throwing and I'll let you go—this time. If you're stupid enough to continue causing trouble and being a pain in the Consortium's ass, I won't be so generous when I catch you next time."

"If you catch me." Luc leaned back as far as he could with his hands behind his back.

"Don't get cute." Dmitri pushed himself upright. "At this point, I could have my officers storm everywhere I know you go, scoop up everyone in there, and send them all to the mines for no other reason than I feel like it. I'm giving you this opportunity because we were friends and because Anna listens to you—for some reason."

Luc saw a crack on the cold floor. It ran to the wall and nearly lined up with a piece of discoloured cement patched over the concrete. He stared at the spot and thought. "She doesn't listen to anyone," he mumbled.

Standing, Dmitri slammed his fist into the table. "She listens to you. She goes out with you on your little pirate runs. She follows you around like a damn puppy."

"You weren't there."

"What did you say?" Dmitri shoved the table to the side and grabbed Luc by his jacket.

Luc looked up at him, still thinking of the city wall. "She followed me because you left."

"I was working! Scraping up enough to keep a

roof over her head!" Spittle flew from his lips and speckled Luc's cheek.

"She wanted you to be there."

Dmitri pushed, tipping the chair back and sending Luc to the floor. "Shut it. Not one more word or the deal is off and your life is over. You'll die in the empty mines, buried so far in the ground that no one will remember you even existed!"

Luc looked up from the floor. "You remember why we did it, don't you?"

Dmitri stared down at him, seething. He breathed heavily through gritted teeth.

"Everything was behind a wall. One copy for one person, at a premium rate." Luc swallowed. "We took it because there was no way we could ever afford it. No one could—other than the wealthy, those with the Consortium. Our parents worked the mines, or served their betters. We ran wild. Took what we needed. Copied digital things. Enough for everyone with nothing lost from those we took it from. But they wanted more. They worked people to death, cleared out the mines and sent them back in to dig deeper. We did what we did—I do what I do, because it's the only way."

Dmitri laughed. "You're a criminal convincing himself he's a hero. You have one chance. Get Anna out of it before I come for you. Tell anyone you want, I don't care. I'll root you all out." He looked up and to the side and the door opened.

The guard who had been standing at the hallway door entered. "Yes, sir."

"Get him out of here."

"Sir?" The guard's shoulders slumped.

Dmitri wiped his hands on his grey pants. "Take off his cuffs and let him go."

"Yes sir." The man picked Luc up, easily hauling him to his feet, and removed the handcuffs.

Luc rubbed his wrists and wiped Dmitri's saliva from his cheek.

"What about his things?" The guard had Luc by the arm, ready to drag him away.

Smiling, Dmitri leaned on the table. "Bring them in here."

As if she had been waiting for the order, the woman in the suit carried the basket into the room and dropped it on the skewed table with a thump.

Dmitri touched her back. "Thank you."

She half smiled and sauntered out of the room, practically slithering around Luc and the guard.

Dumping the basket into the table, Dmitri rummaged through the contents. He picked up the pocket computer and held it up, examining it. "Looks like you put together an upgrade." Squinting one eye, he turned it around in the air before holding it out between Luc and himself. "Not bad." He dropped it and stomped on the pieces. "Not as good as my new toy, though."

Going back to the pile of Luc's things, he set aside the keys and wallet. "These you can keep, but these," he picked up the micro-discs, "I'm afraid you're going to show up empty handed back at the clubhouse tonight." Cracking each one in half, he dropped them onto the remains of the computer. "He can have the rest."

Waving his hand over the table, Dmitri frowned at Luc. "This could have been easy. Talk to Anna."

He left and Luc heard him talking to the woman in the suit. The other door opened and closed and their voices were gone.

The guard pushed Luc towards the table. "Get your crap."

Scooping up his keys and wallet, Luc stuffed them in his pockets. He put on his watch and grabbed his music player. He tried to keep himself from snatching it, from drawing any attention to it. Looking over his shoulder, he saw the guard engaged in some projection produced by his implant. A private image only he could see.

"Hurry up."

Luc put his headphones around his neck and bent down to get the remains of his computer.

"Not that!" The guard grabbed him by the scruff and pulled him to the door.

Scrambling to get his feet under him, Luc

scowled. "Hey."

Two of the soldiers who had brought Luc in were sitting on the desks, the still typing employees clearly annoyed. They stood and joined the man not wearing his helmet.

"What's going on?" the man asked, putting his hand out to stop the guard.

The guard pushed past him. "Out of the way, the director is letting him go."

"That's bullshit. He's our collar. We had to go out in the damn rain to find that prick and we want the arrest."

"I don't care what you want. The director gave the order." The guard pulled Luc behind him, still grabbing his arm. "Is there going to be a problem?"

One of the soldiers stepped in front of his friend. "Come on. It's not worth it. Let's go complain to the captain."

"I don't know that I want to let it go."

The guard made a low sound, like a growl. "Listen to your friend."

Luc laughed. "Are you guys serious? Is this the kind of pissing match you assholes get into working for the man?"

Throwing his elbow back, the guard knocked Luc to the ground.

Wiping his mouth, Luc saw blood on his hand. "Good one."

"Get up."

Sighing, Luc got to his feet. The guard pushed him out of the room and down the hallway. The soldiers seemed to have given up. As they entered the scanning room on the city side of the wall, Luc went to leave, but the guard pulled him back.

"This again?"

There was an old man behind an identical metal desk as the woman who had scanned him in. He pointed at the scanner, a stone-faced scowl etched into his features.

Luc huffed and put his face to the screen. The lights crisscrossed and the device beeped cheerily.

Before he could straighten, the guard pulled him back and shoved him out the door. Luc tripped, rolled once, and landed, splayed on the muddy ground.

"Thank you."

The guard was gone. Another group of soldiers working the city side laughed, their helmets muffling the sound. One of them gave Luc a kick.

"Come on. Out of here, scrub. Past the line."

Luc got to his feet, again, and left the border area. He opened his music player and took out the copy of the broadcast.

Broadcast Wasteland

Six
Encircled

A red line painted on the cracked pavement marked out a do-not-cross zone at the checkpoint. The street leading to the massive doors was twice as wide as the ones in the rest of the city, as was the sidewalk that was separated from it by a metal railing. The buildings on either side, built right up against the city wall, were a couple of stories taller than it, enclosing the space. The low storm clouds were like a ceiling over top, but the constant rain ruined the illusion.

Luc pulled his jacket tight to keep out the water and turned right at the first street. He checked his watch. It was twenty past two in the morning. The dials on the watch still worked, but the small, rectangular screen was blank without a connection to his computer. Groaning at the thought, Luc made a mental note to get his backup on his way to the diner.

Broadcast Wasteland

There were no people wandering around the streets near the wall, and only a few cars passed him along the circular road that went around the whole city. The short buildings were mostly apartments with shops on the ground floor—half of them boarded up or abandoned. Streetlights made bright patches on both sides of the street, blending in with the lights on the wall that shone between buildings. A few bioengineered trees, planted in rectangles of dirt surrounded by concrete and stone, rustled as the wind picked up. It carried the rain sideways into Luc's face. He reached a main artery and took it, heading farther into the city. Within a couple of blocks, the apartments got shorter and older and a few single-use buildings and offices were mixed in. The streetlights got more spotty, too, some of them broken with remnants of glass scattered below them.

Luc reached his building, a five-story walk-up with a crumbling stoop and layers of graffiti across the front. He opened the broken outer door and un-locked the heavy-duty inner one. It slammed shut loudly behind him. He headed down the creaking wooden stairs to his basement unit—one of four. They were slightly larger than the others, but, other than flimsy walls around the bathroom, were single open rooms.

Unlocking three deadbolts and a chain, he slipped inside and sloughed off his wet jacket. He threw it over the back of a dining room chair and peeled off his soaked hoodie and shirt. The apartment was mostly taken up by three mismatched desks in a 'u' shape, covered in various computers, parts, and half started projects. One was dedicated to a large Hamm radio with cracked lenses over the vu meters. The metal housing was sitting next to the unit with a box of spare tubes on top of it. Luc bypassed it and opened the drawer of a filing cabinet under the centre desk. He pulled out his backup pocket computer, battered with a half dead battery and a missing 'w' key. He turned it on and plugged it into the breadbox-like main computer on his desk, setting it to update.

He thought of the data he was missing from the computer Dmitri had smashed, but it was just from the previous day's update. The real prize was the micro-disc he still had in his music player.

While the pocket computer updated, Luc found another shirt in a pile of, probably, clean laundry. The logo of his favourite parts manufacturer, Mahoney Semiconductor, was plastered across the front in orange letters. He pulled it on and noticed multiple messages waiting for him on the desktop, all from Anna.

Smirking, he waited for the update to finish, grabbed the replacement pocket computer and picked up his jacket. There was a puddle of water under the chair where it had been. Luc took hold of it by the sleeves and shook it before slipping it back on. A few spots on his back were still wet, but he ignored it, stuck the computer into an inner pocket and headed back out the door.

His watch automatically connected as he left his building, vibrating to remind him of his waiting messages. Ignoring it, he headed back towards the city centre and cut down an alley. He noticed a man sleeping under a wet blanket, his cardboard home caved in from the rain. Luc tossed a few Consortium coins on the ground next to him without stopping. The temperature was dropping and he could see his breath. Crossing the next street, he spotted The Royal Diner, the interior lights shining through the big windows and spilling out onto the dark street.

A few people were hanging out near the door, most of them smoking, one doing something with a little tin of powder that Luc couldn't quite make out. The group was all young, early-to-mid twenties and a few teenagers. A chill made Luc shudder and the general ache in his legs and back was acute.

A girl wearing a leather jacket with little metal spikes clustered on her shoulders, left the awning and jogged up to him with bouncing steps.

"Hey there, Luc. Got anything you can share?" She had her hands in her pockets and looked up at him, her chin tucked into her chest, forcing doe eyes.

"Not tonight, Sasha." Luc tried to side step her, but she got in front of him.

"Oh, come on. Not even for me?" She pouted, her dark red lipstick partially rubbed off.

Luc stopped and furrowed his brow. "I've got the new broadcast if you can wait for me to compile it."

Sasha took her hand out of her pocket and ran a finger down his jacket. "That's not what I'm talking about and you know it."

"You should go home. Don't let Skeeter and his boys take advantage of you." Pushing past her, Luc stared at a young man leaning against the adjacent building. He had a cigarette hanging out of his mouth and his spiked hair was flattened under the rain. The guy pulled a lower eyelid down, and someone in the group around him laughed like a hyena.

"Screw you, Luc," Sasha said. "I just need some cash, not a lecture."

"I'm not some suit you can hustle. If you're going to manipulate people, you should get better at it." Luc pulled open the door to the diner and went in.

Broadcast Wasteland

Seven
Almost Coffee

The few people in the diner filled the dining room with sparse chatter. An old Earth song played over speakers in the ceiling, and the smell of cooking grease stuck to everything. Anna hopped off a stool at the counter and hurried over to him.

Luc put up his hands. "I know."

As soon as she was in range, she punched his shoulder. Her head stopped at his chin, so she had to punch up. "I've been waiting here for over an hour. I thought you'd been caught."

"I was."

Anna's mouth hung open. Her black ponytail swung as she shook her head. The oversized cable knit sweater she wore was damp and the sleeves kept slipping over her hands. "You can't joke about that."

A large man, taller than Luc and twice as wide, sauntered up to them on the other side of the counter. He wiped his hands on his stained apron. "You want a coffee, Luc?"

Avoiding Anna's gaze, Luc nodded to the man. "Yes please, Jean. And, can I have a special?"

Jean put his hands on his hips. "It's a little early."

"I'm going to be here a while."

Turning, Jean grabbed a pot of coffee off the burner and a mug from under the counter. He placed the steaming mug on the Formica surface with a clack, spilling a little of the liquid over the side, marking the white surface. "You slip me a copy of whatever you get and I'll start on the potatoes."

Luc smiled. "You're the best, Jean."

Anna stepped in front of him. "Stop ignoring me and tell me what happened."

Nodding to the counter and the waiting coffee, Luc took a seat. He sipped at the hot liquid and shuddered. "I wish we could get the real stuff. This synthetic junk is too bitter."

Anna sat next to him. "Then put some sugar in it. Quit stalling."

Putting the mug down, Luc took out his pocket computer and the micro-disc from the music player and started the decoding process on the broadcast he'd intercepted.

"Why are you using your old machine?" Anna grabbed his arm and her face sank. "Tell me what happened."

Luc cleared his throat. "I was spotted by those ships. They chased me off the tower and I was surrounded by soldiers in the market. I managed to hide in that secret hatch by the old lady's stall, but they got me as soon as I was out in the open. I wasn't expecting the buildings to be all torn down."

Anna scrunched up her forehead. "Yeah. That was so fast. It was almost as if they were doing it to catch us."

"How'd you get through?" Luc took another sip. He heard sizzling from the window to the grill in the back and could smell onions frying.

Shrugging, Anna grabbed Luc's mug and swigged some of the coffee. She puckered her mouth at the taste. "Don't know. I didn't see anyone and the lady at the checkpoint just waved me through."

Luc sighed. He leaned over the counter and reached under the far side to grab another mug. "It's your brother."

"Don't start with that again!"

Standing, he stretched out for the coffee pot and filled the new mug. "I'm serious. He's in charge of some taskforce. They hauled me in and we had a little chat in an interrogation room."

"A chat about what?"

Luc looked away. "About you mostly. He let me go so I could talk you into quitting, or out of hacking, or whatever."

"That son-of-a—when I get my—"

"Don't." Luc squinted at her.

"What?"

"Do whatever you're thinking. This is serious. He said he's coming down on all of us and I believe him. I'm sure he was the one behind clearing the slums and tearing them down. He knew to search for us tonight and he's made it nearly impossible for us, for anyone, to get out of the city anymore. He's intent on taking the broadcast away and sending as many hackers to the mines as he can. You've got a chance to avoid it." Luc smiled. "Plus, I'm sure he got a big raise with the title. Has an implant and everything. You won't even need to scrape and scrounge anymore."

"Ugh." She hit him in the shoulder again, but lighter. "You're full of crap, you know that?"

"How?"

Anna swivelled on her stool to face him. "You know I have no interest in the Consortium's money unless we're taking it from them."

Luc shushed her and glanced around the diner.

"Relax." She waved a hand at him. "My brother is an ass. I don't care what he thinks or what he decides for me."

"Your brother isn't an ass. He's doing what he thinks is right. He's trying to be there for you. You should cut him some slack."

"He abandoned me to go work for those monsters. And I'm not some spineless, helpless waif who does what she's told. Not from him and not from you." She pulled up the sleeves on her sweater. "Besides, you could just as easily abandon all this as I could. Spare his wrath."

Luc shook his head and took another sip. "He's got it out for me. I'm sure we're all on some list anyway. He'll take you off it. I'll hang if I quit or not."

Anna grabbed his sleeve. "Then let's go."

"Oh, sure. We'll just hop into my rocket and blast off to some other planet." He tugged his arm away. "Or, we'll magically get our hands on some papers and just take the next corporate shuttle off world—in a year or three."

Anna bit her lip. "You know that's not what I'm talking about."

Jean lumbered around the corner, a large plate in hand. He placed it down in front of Luc and a sausage nearly rolled away. Eggs, sausage, home fries, toast, the plate was overloaded. The smell hit Luc and he leaned into it, eyes closed.

"Thanks, Jean. It's exactly what I needed."

"Uh huh. And how's the broadcast coming?" The large man leaned on the counter with one thick arm and the surface flexed.

Luc checked the progress on his computer. "It's

coming."

The big cook turned and headed back towards the kitchen. "It better be. And that's not free, neither."

"I know."

The man disappeared around the corner and appeared at the window. "And don't think I missed that coffee. I ought to charge you extra for helping yourself."

Luc shrugged. "I didn't want to bother you."

"Uh huh." Jean looked over at Anna. "How you doing sweetie?"

"I'm good, thanks."

"How about a slice of pie."

Anna shook her head. "I'm okay."

"It'll be on him." Jean nodded towards Luc.

Smiling, Anna leaned on her elbows. "Okay, then."

Luc huffed. "How come he gets to call you sweetie?"

"It's endearing." Anna grabbed the coffee cup in both hands. "And I'm not done with you."

Luc picked up a fork and started on a sausage. "I have no doubt."

"I think we should go wherever the broadcasts are coming from. You've talked about it before. Now's the perfect time." Anna focused on the liquid in the mug.

Luc stopped mid-bite. "We talked about it the same way we've talked about going to Earth or joining Telbak. Unrealistic dreams."

"Amcoral."

"What?"

"I'd rather join Amcoral."

Sighing, Luc noticed that the broadcast had stopped compiling. "You got the blank discs?"

Without looking, Anna reached into a backpack at her feet and pulled out a box of mismatched micro-discs. She dropped it on the counter in between them. "What are our options?"

Luc slid the box closer to the computer. He ejected his master disc, putting it back into his music player, and inserted the first blank, starting the copy program. "I wonder what stuff they embedded in the signal this week."

"Stop avoiding my question."

Digging into his potatoes, Luc grabbed the nearest bottle of hot sauce and glugged some onto his plate. "You move back in with your brother full time, find some respectable job, go take some classes at the corporate college. Maybe find a way off this planet."

"And you?" She reached over and took a pieces of toast. She stuck it in her mouth and slid his computer in front of her, putting in another disc to copy.

"I'll keep at this until no one is allowed outside

the city anymore. Maybe find a new place to hijack the signal. Helmut thinks he found a spot on the far side of the city, near the spaceport."

"You hate Helmut. And you said it yourself. My brother is coming for you." Anna took a bite.

"Then I get a job in some repair shop, fixing net-boxes for Corporate spouses. Or, I could always get a job at the recycling plant."

She poked his hand with the remnants of the toast. "You'll lose a finger in there. Besides, we'd both be miserable. All our friends will be forced to work in the mines and you know Dmitri." Putting the crust down on his plate, she took his hand in hers. "He'll never stop trying. He probably already has a file with enough stuff to arrest you."

Luc picked up the crust with his free hand and placed it on the counter. "Our situations stem from the same person. They're fixed. You have a chance to get away with no repercussions. I don't. I'm not going to let you throw that away because you're worried about me."

Anna replaced the disc again, stacking the new copy on the first one. "Well, you're not going to get rid of me. If you keep doing this, so will I."

"Then I'll stop."

A chime went off as the door opened and three people the same age as the punks hanging out in front of the restaurant came in. One guy was gently pushing his friend away from the door while a woman walked around them and up to Anna.

"Hey, we heard you got the new broadcast already."

"Hi Gretchen. How'd you hear that so fast?" Anna switched the discs again, handing the fresh copy to the girl.

Gretchen nodded to the kitchen. "Jean put the word out. Andrei's been keeping an eye on the message boards."

"We're just copying it now. No idea what's on them yet. You got the creds?"

The two guys made it to the counter. Gretchen put her arm around the one who needed to be held back. "Andrei, pay up."

Andrei kept looking out the front window. "Yeah." He handed her some coins.

"Let it go," Gretchen said as she passed the credits over to Anna.

"I swear I'm going to put that Skeeter in the ground one of these days."

The other guy rolled his eyes and moved next to Anna. "Sasha's out there pushing hard. Andrei told her off and Skeeter flipped." He handed over his credits and took the next disc out of the computer.

Anna frowned. "He'll mess you up, Andrei. He doesn't fight fair and his buddies will jump in as soon as your back is turned. You'd be lucky just to get stabbed."

"That's what I said."

Luc dropped his fork. It clanked off his plate, cutting the conversation. "Do you mind?"

"Sorry, boss," Andrei said. "That guy just gets my blood boiling."

"Look." Luc swivelled on the stool. "I appreciate you're excited for a copy of the broadcast. I'm grateful that you come to me and actually pay for it instead of just getting it off the net in a few days, but I haven't even looked at what's on it yet. I'll be pulling files and messages out of the code for days still."

"We know, boss. We just get excited. Plus, Leon there likes to try to crack it himself. He's pretty good."

Luc looked over at Anna, his eyebrows furrowed. "Where did this boss stuff come from?"

A smile cracked on her face. "They respect you."

"We do," Leon said. "Your copies are the best and you always find the most code in the stream."

"Get a room," Gretchen said, laughing.

Leon turned to her, pointing a finger. "You want to go out into the slums and hack a tower? I didn't think so."

Luc put up his hands. "Okay. I'm glad you're happy. Can I go back to eating?"

Gretchen pulled Andrei towards an open booth.

"Oooh. I want waffles."

"Then you should pay for them."

She checked him with her hip as they squeezed into one side.

Leon hesitated. "Hey, you think some time I can go out with you and Anna? Like, just to watch?"

Luc scratched an eyebrow. "Probably not. They're tearing down the slums as we speak. I'm not sure where we're going to get the next broadcast from."

"Oh." Leon looked at his feet. "Okay. I hope you figure it out."

"Me too, kid." Luc picked up his fork and went back to his breakfast.

Turning to Anna, Leon stuffed his hands in his pockets. "Uh, Anna?"

"Yeah?" Anna was busy copying discs, the finished pile growing.

"You want to have some waffles with us?"

Anna took a sharp breath. "I'm, uh, a little busy with this—but thanks."

"Okay. Maybe some other time."

"Yeah. Maybe."

Leon headed for the booth and Gretchen made woo sounds as he sat.

Luc brought his mug up to his mouth but stopped before taking a drink. "Why didn't you go get waffles with your friends?"

"I'm working." Anna didn't look at him.

"I can do that." Luc put the mug down and reached for the computer.

Anna slapped his hand. "I can do it. Besides. We're not done talking."

Eight
Morning

Anna put her fork down on the small plate smeared with the red remnants of the cherry pie. Pale light from the ultra-cool red dwarf TRAPPIST 1 washed over the city wall and snaked its way through the streets. The gang that had been hanging out in front of the diner had dispersed, but more customers were trickling in to replace them. Among the young punks were blue-collar workers starting their long day and the odd corporate employee in suits marked with red and black accents.

Several of the patrons had purchased discs from Luc and Anna, some of them making the trip specifically to get their hands on the latest broadcast. Others purchased it out of convenience, including more than one Consortium employee.

The stack of discs on the counter was dwindling and Luc finished his fourth cup of coffee. The box of blanks Anna had brought was empty, the copying done for the day.

Jean took the pie plate, a smile on his whiskered face. "And how was that, sweetie?"

"Delicious as always, Jean. I don't know how your brother manages to make such good desserts with imitation ingredients, but they're the best in the city."

The cook chuckled. "Don't tell him that, it'll go to his head." Sidestepping, Jean stood in front of Luc. "Well?"

Stifling a yawn, Luc glared up at the big man. "You got your copy, right?"

"Yup."

"And it looks like some of your customers are people who came here to see me and stayed for breakfast."

"Seems that way."

Luc scratched his head. "You're welcome."

"You still owe me for the food, and the coffee. Plus a tip for not breaking your arm after you reached over my counter to help yourself."

Throwing up his hands, Luc sat up. "I told you, I didn't want to bother you." He dug into his pockets, the coins collected over the early morning jingling against each other. "You could give me a bill like a normal person." He dropped a fistful of coins on the counter, one or two of them rolling away.

Anna snatched them before they could go over the edge.

"That enough?" Luc asked.

Jean dropped a large hand on the Formica and shovelled the coins into his other oversized mitt. "That should do."

"It's highway robbery." Luc pulled out the rest of the collected credits, counting them out in his open hand. "I have to pay rent with this, Jean." He split them into two piles and handed one over to Anna.

Bending down low, Jean leaned close to Luc's face. "You're lucky I let you use my restaurant to do your shady business."

"Yeah, you're a saint." Luc grabbed his pocket computer and stuck it into his jacket. He spun on the stool and got up.

Jean handed Anna a Styrofoam container. "An extra slice of pie for the road."

Anna took the to-go box and patted the cook's hand. "You're the best, Jean."

Luc headed for the door. Andrei, Gretchen, and Leon were still in their booth, all of them listening to the micro-discs they had bought from him—Andrei and Gretchen sharing a pair of headphones. Leon noticed Luc leaving and stopped his player.

"Excellent decoding, boss."

Stopping at the doorway, Luc sighed before

looking back. "Thanks."

"Hey, uh. If I dig up some content in the code, you think I could send it your way? Like, maybe I'll get to something before you do and it'll save you some time?"

Anna caught up to Luc. She held up the container Jean had given her and smiled.

"Goodbye, Anna. Maybe next time we can get those waffles," Leon said.

"Later, Leon. Stay out of trouble." She waved at him.

The sun crested the city wall and a ray shone through the window, making Luc squint. "Why don't you go ahead and send me what you find. If you beat me to something, I'll give you credit in the notes."

Leon beamed brighter than the weak sun. "Yeah? Thanks, boss. I'll get on it right now!"

Luc pushed open the door and walked out. The morning chill permeated everything. The storm that had assaulted him hours earlier was gone, just a few of the clouds coloured the sky, but the street was still damp. Moisture hung in the air. The terraforming machines were more than enough for the small planet, but far from top-of-the-line. With the cool sun keeping the temperature just on the lower end of comfortable, the machines the size of the city spread along the equator worked at full capacity to make the atmosphere habitable.

Still, even though it was technically the summer, Luc zipped up his jacket. Anna bounced out after him and hugged herself.

"Brr." Wisps of breath puffed out of her mouth. "It's going to be a cold day."

Luc headed down the sidewalk. It was still early, but businesses were opening and some pedestrians were going about their morning. A few cars rolled by silently, early morning go-getters looking to make a mark in the corporation, Luc thought.

"I'm going home. I'm spent."

Anna caught up with him. "We didn't finish talking."

"I'm finished." Luc stopped. "You should head home. I'm sure Dmitri is waiting up for you."

"I'm not giving up on this, Luc." Anna had grabbed the ends of her sleeves and balled them up in her fists, covering her hands under the oversized sweater, the takeout container stuffed into her bag. "We should leave, today. Tomorrow at the latest. Get out while we can."

Luc sniffed. He could feel the cold numbing his nose. "I'm not going, but I'll make you a promise." He looked up and watched a recycling truck glide around the corner. It stopped at the first store. A woman hopped off the back and started emptying bins. A man slid out from behind the driver's seat and helped her.

"I'll stop." Luc looked back at Anna. She was standing close to him. "If you promise to try to do what your brother wants—to do something with this opportunity, I'll stop. This will be my last broadcast."

Anna stepped closer, nearly pressing up against him. "Really?"

"I'll start looking for a job tomorrow. I've got a few friends who owe me favours." He half-smiled. "Besides, I can still do some decoding on the sly, and maybe even do some work on those programs I've been talking about since we were in school."

"What if my brother comes after you anyway?" She leaned her head against his chest.

Luc sighed and let his chin rest on top of her. "If you fall in line, at least a little, and I stop breaking the law, he'll have no reason to. He may even cut me some slack for getting you to play along."

"But, you'll be miserable. Getting the broadcast from Helmut. Working some crappy job for less than what you make now."

Taking Anna by the shoulders, Luc put distance between them. "That doesn't matter. I couldn't do it forever anyway."

Anna took a deep breath. The sun was crawling up the sky, dissipating the moisture from the air. "Okay." She nodded once. "I'll play my part, but you have to keep thinking about leaving—and you have to just sit there and listen when I bring it up."

Slipping from his grasp, she wrapped her arms around him. "And you have to keep spending time with me. No getting busy and drifting apart."

Luc huffed as she squeezed. "Okay."

"Promise." She let him go.

"Sure. I promise." Luc stifled another yawn. "But right now, I'm going to bed."

Anna held out her sleeve-covered hand. Luc put out his own and she dropped the credits he had given to her. "I don't want these," she said, her face scrunched.

She turned and headed towards the nicer buildings at the city center. "I'll message you after we've had a nap, tell you how Dmitri reacts."

Broadcast Wasteland

Nine
Voices

Luc closed the door to his apartment and flipped all the locks. He hadn't seen anyone from the building coming or going and assumed the few residents who had a job were already gone. The puddle under the chair was still there, but smaller, and the smell of one of his neighbours cooking filled the air. Blackout shades were drawn over the small windows, but light was beaming around their edges, giving the room a twilight feel.

Dropping his jacket on the same chair, Luc took his pocket computer and music player to his desk. He plugged the dying computer into the larger desktop unit, simultaneously transferring the data and charging the smaller device.

The bar that indicated the transfer moved quickly and as soon as the broadcast file was on the desktop it opened in a program that let Luc read the code. He scrolled to the bottom without sitting, looking for the author signature. His was the last line of the document, *captured and compiled by Luc*. Just above that was a symbol, concentric circles spreading out from a tiny solar system matching TRAPPIST. It was the same mark on every broadcast and though there was endless speculation, no one knew who the creators of the broadcast were.

Absentmindedly scrolling through the code, Luc picked out a few sections that looked like they could be messages or tiny applications. He copied them and dropped them into another program he'd built that would compile them just as they did the data for the broadcast itself.

He yawned, his mouth opening so widely his jaw cracked. "Damn. That chase wore me out."

Leaving the program running, he scooped up his music player and trundled to his bed. He dropped the device on the mattress and walked around it to the kitchen. Grabbing a chipped glass off the counter, he opened the tap, letting the water run until it was mostly clear. The colony ran on recycled water mixed with what ice Consortium ships could find in the rest of the solar system. The rain generated by the terraforming complexes was clean enough to bathe in, but only the people who used to live in the slums were desperate enough to drink it untreated. Even in his part of the city, Luc knew they received more recycled water than fresh.

Filling the glass, he chugged the water, gasping while he let it fill up again. Closing the faucet, he took more measured sips as he went back to the bed. Placing the glass on the side table, he kicked off his shoes, pants, and socks, and dropped onto the mattress—the micro-disc player bouncing into his side. Luc put the headphones on, pressed play, and pulled the comforter over his head.

A series of tones played through the small speakers pressed against his ears. They morphed into a tune that marked the start of the broadcast. A robotic voice read snippets of extrasolar news over the music.

The colonization of Gliese was in jeopardy as both Amcoral and Telbak were making claims on key landing sites. A skirmish between two smaller corporations over rights to rare minerals in a distant, uninhabited system was spreading. A researcher examining data from a probe's trip to a new star claimed to find signs of an extinct alien civilization and her corporation was covering up the findings.

Luc chuckled and rolled onto his side. He knew the news he got from the Consortium outlet was at best propaganda, but even though the broadcast kept him informed about real happenings in the human explored sections of the galaxy, they were too keen with news about aliens.

He drifted off by the time the show got to the new music section.

Luc woke and shot out of bed, tripping over the comforter he pulled with him, crashing to the floor. The headphones he was wearing were hanging halfway off his head, the left speaker over his eye. Extricating himself from the blankets, he remembered snippets of the dream he'd been having.

The colony was in ruins. Ice covered everything, creeping in from the wastelands. Ships were launching but he was in the mine, cold to the bone, surrounded by bodies. Then a familiar voice spoke to him and he felt bright warmth.

Luc shook his head and squinted. He straightened the headphones still thinking of the voice that woke him.

"The voice!"

Pulling on the cord in his hands, he reeled in the music player and fumbled for the rewind button. The words ran backwards at triple speed.

Letting go, the broadcast continued. There was a human voice—no—multiple voices overlapping. The words were a jumble. Luc thought he could make out 'us' and 'travel'. Everything else was undecipherable. He could have sworn he heard someone telling him to go to them. Pulling off the headphones, he rubbed his eyes.

There was still light coming in through the edges of the blinds, but dimly and at a sharper angle. He checked his watch. It was two in the afternoon. Leaning on the edge of the bed, he grabbed the glass of water and drained it. Standing, he plodded to the bathroom that jutted out into the space, passing his desktop computer on the way.

Something caught his eye and stopped him in his tracks. "Come to us?"

He dropped into the chair and opened the message that had been decoded from the broadcast file.

Now is the time. Dear listeners, supporters, believers. We are out there waiting for you. Come to us. You know the way. Together we can save this world and give it to those who deserve it—the people who toil to make it a home. We have a way to drive out the Consortium and make a new, free TRAPPIST. Come to us.

Luc's mouth hung open. "Come to us."

Closing the window, Luc sent a message to Anna. His fingers flew across the keyboard as he wrote about listening to the recording, his dream, and the message. He told her he was going to get a new pocket computer and that she should meet him at the used electronics store where a hacker they knew worked. He thought of Dmitri, the look on the man's face when he found out that not only was Luc going to disobey his orders, but was joining a group of people who were actively working against the Consortium. Luc chuckled as he hit send.

His finger froze on the key as something struck him. Anna. In his excitement, Luc sent her the message without thinking about what she would be giving up.

"Shit." He stood and stared at the screen with no way to stop the message that had already made it to a satellite and back down to wherever she was in the moment.

"I should have just left." Luc kicked the chair. "She'd find me and kill me if I didn't say goodbye." He let his shoulders drop and the smile faded. Chewing on his lip, he worked the problem and headed for the bathroom, stripping off his shirt on the way.

Ten
Like Spokes in a Wheel

The small sun was high in the sky, but the city still felt grey. Most of the buildings, especially any of the newer ones the Consortium had hastily erected when they took over the colony, were made of concrete and the rocks discarded from mining.

The used electronics shop was on one of the main arteries that ran like spokes from the centre of the city to the checkpoints surrounding it. The fastest way from Luc's apartment was to head downtown and cut across where the spokes were closer together, but Luc kept away from downtown when he could. There were too many corporate employees, too many soldiers. Instead, he took the circuitous route through the poorer neighbourhoods.

Keeping his head down, he walked at a brisk pace through the rundown side streets, noting the increase in graffiti on the buildings, signs, and electrical poles. The colours were overwhelmingly yellow and purple. Prominently drawn in the middle of most of the markings was a simple depiction of an oblong face with a tiki-like grin and a little crown.

There were a lot of street gangs in the small city, most like Skeeter and his handful of drug addicts and misfits. Some of the hackers Luc knew were tied to the gangs in one way or another. Helmut, his main competition in distributing the broadcast, ran with the Trappers in the opposite wedge of city from Luc's neighbourhood but the tag he was seeing on everything in front of him was from the CreeperK-ings.

The graffiti gradually cleared by the time he reached the shop in the late afternoon. The prominent purple and yellow was surrounded by a rainbow of other colours sprayed on top of each other so many times that no one symbol or word was discernible.

The store was at the end of a side street on the main floor of a building that could otherwise be a cousin of the one he lived in. There was no sign indicating the name of the place, but 'Used Parts' was painted on the glass door with a jagged burst around it. The front window had bars on the outside and the interior was so stuffed with shelves and components that it looked closed at first.

Luc stopped with his hand on the door handle,

the unresolved problem of messaging Anna demanding attention before he went inside. He boiled things down to two possibilities. They left together and she gave up on her future, or he ran off on his own and he took away her agency—and potentially hurt her.

Biting his lip, he pulled the door open. It was her decision to make.

A few bare fluorescent tubes buzzed on the ceiling of the shop, casting a bluish light that failed to reach into the corners. Rows of metal shelves nearly to the ceiling ran the length of the space to the left of the doorway. Prebuilt computers ranging from pocket models to desktops and full server setups were displayed on the right wall. A counter covered in parts and tools blocked off a door farther back.

As Luc approached, he noticed an old man lounging in a chair by the door. His mostly bald head peeked over the top of the counter. The man had a handkerchief over his face, the corner dancing along with his wheezing breaths.

Luc found a bell amidst the things on the counter and slapped it. The ring blasted out sharply and trailed off. The man sat up, coughing.

"What the hell?" He pulled the handkerchief from his face and looked up at Luc, his eyebrows crossed.

"Augustus. You shouldn't be sleeping on the

job." Luc pressed his lips together and shook his head. "If I were an unscrupulous man, I could have robbed this place blind."

Pulling himself out of the chair, Augustus glared at Luc and pressed a button under the countertop. Metal bars slid in front of the door, clanking as they settled into place. The lights went out and were replaced by a red, pulsing flash and sirens.

Luc covered his ears and squinted. "You made your point!"

Augustus pressed the button again and things went back to normal so quickly, Luc second-guessed that that it had happened at all.

The old man licked his lips. "You try and take anything without going through me, and you get to wait in here for security." He stuffed the handkerchief into the breast pocket of his polo shirt. The dark stripes over the off-white material were faded and old stains were scattered all over it and his brown pants. He was thin and hunched, but stood solidly.

"I was just making a point." Luc pushed a circuit board aside and leaned on the counter. "I'm here to see Berlin."

"Who?"

Luc scrunched his face. "I don't have time to play any games, Gus. Do you really not remember, or are you trying to be coy?"

"M'I supposed to know you?" Augustus leaned

closer, his red nose nearly touching Luc's.

"I'd hope so. I've done enough business here." Luc looked over his shoulder to the systems on the wall. "By the way. I'm in the market for a new pocket model. My good one was smashed by a Consortium lackey and my backup has seen better days. Got anything Terra based? I'm partial to Mahoney chipsets."

The old man huffed and knocked on the door behind him. "I think this one's for you, Tri." With a grunt, Augustus lifted the hinged end of the counter so Luc could come through. "Make sure to keep it down. I'm trying to get some rest."

"I'll keep that in mind." Luc tried the handle on the back door, but it was locked. A speaker buzzed overhead.

"Look up and into the camera and state your name." The voice was tinny and hollow.

Luc stared into the old camera hanging from the ceiling. It moved to focus on him, whirling. "It's Luc."

"State your handle please?"

Luc slumped his shoulders. "Come on, Tri. Please don't make me."

The voice over the speaker fought a fit of laughter. "Rules are rules. I need your official handle."

Sighing, Luc closed his eyes. "RadDude."

"I'll need the whole thing if I'm going to let you in."

"RadDude sixty-nine." Luc bit on the words, his jaw tight.

The door clicked and opened. "You may enter, RadDude."

Luc pushed his way into the back, slamming the door behind him. "I get that I chose a stupid handle when I was a kid. It's not my fault I was good enough for it to stick."

The back room was windowless. The only light other than a single bulb on the ceiling came from dozens of computer monitors. They were mostly stacked on top of each other against the far wall sitting on a desk that jutted out into the room. A big wooden spool sat on its side acting as a table in front of a ratty old couch. A red exit sign glowed over a door on the left wall. Computer fans whirred along with pedestal fans that blew around the warm air.

Tri was leaning back in her chair, laughing. She wore an oversized sleeveless shirt halfway off her shoulder but no pants. "Ladies and gentlemen. The one, the only, RadDude!" She clapped and whistled.

"You know, if you had a window back here it wouldn't be so warm and you wouldn't have to be half naked." Luc raised his eyebrows.

Tri stood and stalked towards him. "Oh. Is the big, bad, Rad, Dude scared of a little skin?" When she got close, she pounced, dropping them both onto the couch. Her long hair cascaded around them. "Oh, no. Now my skin is actually touching you! What's a woman to do?" She rolled off of him, the back of her hand on her forehead, pretending to swoon.

Luc tried not to laugh. "I'm just saying, it's hot in here. You could put in some ventilation or something."

Settling on the couch, Tri crossed her legs. "I don't need no Consortium Operative spying on me. This room is on total lock down. I sealed the vents and coated the walls in RF blocking foil."

"No little foil hat?" Luc pulled off his jacket. "What're you running right now?"

Tri shrugged. "All kinds of things. I'm scanning traffic in the sector, collecting data on incoming and outgoing shipments. Dug up a bunch of dirt on some officers and officials." Pulling her hair back, she leaned on her arm. "Not sure what I want to do with that. Right now, I'm trying to figure out some odd traffic that's been clogging up my scans. I keep getting conflicting information and there's a ton of noise on the network. Some of it I haven't been able to decode."

"Huh." Luc scrunched his face. "The download last night was bogged down too."

Tri snorted. "Seems like the Consortium is having troubles. The space station isn't even connected to the network right now." She pointed to one of the screens that showed a scrolling list of network nodes.

"Good. They deserve all the problems they get. I take it you've given up on broadcast running?"

"You cornered that market." Tri poked him in the chest. "Even Helmut started using your copies and uploading them as his own."

Luc sat up. "Since when?"

Tri blew out a breath, her lips vibrating. "How long have you been intercepting the signals from the towers in the middle of the night?"

Sitting back, Luc scratched his head. Sweat was building around his hairline. "Not my fault I care about quality."

"Care? You're obsessed, dude." Tri smiled. "Rad-Dude."

"Hey, you hear anything about what's going on with the CreeperKings?"

Tri shrugged. "Not much other than that they're expanding. They took their neighbourhood in a rush, wiping out their competition in the biblical way. They've been raiding the neighbourhoods around them. I'm surprised you haven't heard about it. You're right next to them, aren't you?"

"Yeah. I had no idea."

"Well, they've been working with the Rancore Siblings."

Luc leaned forward. "Seriously?"

"Not sure how they hooked up, but with that kind of hacking prowess, they were able to take their territory in record time. Probably only keep away from you because you crashed the Sibling's systems so many times. That, and you broke Alexi's nose."

"He swung at me first." Luc shifted on the couch.

"That's what they get for trying to muscle in on your precious broadcast, right? Not like anyone's going to beat you to the punch if you keep raiding the towers."

"Actually, that's kind of why I'm here."

Tri stood. "Here we go. What can I do for you?"

"There's a bunch, actually, but I need to start by giving you a warning." Luc peered at her, his mouth tight.

"Getting into the racketeering business?"

Luc shook his head. "Just passing along the one I got." He looked away, grimacing at nothing. "Dmitri got a promotion. He's head of a special operation—"

"—that traitor couldn't operate his way out of his own pants." Tri crossed her arms.

"He's coming, Tri, for all of us. He caught me last night, dragged me into an interrogation room."

Tri shoved her desk chair away. It rolled into one of the fans with a clang. She leaned over her desk, typing furiously. "Are you kidding me? You got caught and you came to me in less than a day? If they get to me, I'm going to cut your dick off, Luc."

Luc walked over to her. "Let me finish. Dmitri told me he's coming for all of us. He's the one who was behind emptying the slums. It's probably all bulldozed by now. They were going at it last night—had a whole ring cleared up against the city wall."

Tri didn't answer. She kept typing, moving from one system to the next.

"Listen to me." Luc tried to grab her arm, but she shrugged him off.

"Listen to what? They probably already burned me. You're definitely being followed. They might even have this place surrounded already." Sidestepping to the end of her desk, she checked a series of monitors, each split into four sections showing footage from the cameras inside and outside the shop.

"I doubt it. He's too cocky for that. He let me go so I could convince Anna to stop."

Looking at him over her shoulder, Tri shook her head. "Of course it has something to do with her. You two always made bad decisions when it came to that girl."

"Triana, will you listen to me for a second!"

Tri shoved him, sending him into the spindle. He fell, knocking over bottles and food containers.

"Back off, or that'll be the least of what I do to

you," she said.

"I'm trying to tell you something. I'm trying to give you a warning of what's coming. You know Dmitri almost as well as I do. He's going to burn this city to the ground to get to us. All of us." Luc sat up, flinging the remains of a drink from his arm. "He gave me a head start so I could talk to Anna. He implied that if I stopped he wouldn't come for me."

"That's bullshit."

"I know. That's what I'm saying. It's over…for all of us."

There was a knock on the door. They booth looked at it, then at the monitor displaying the camera image of the person on the other side. It was Anna.

Tri gritted her teeth. "Oh, this is going to be great."

Broadcast Wasteland

Eleven
Calmer Heads

Tri stomped over to a filing cabinet next to the couch and grabbed a pair of pants that were draped over it.

"What are you doing?" Luc stood and watched her.

Sliding the pants on, Tri went back to her desk, pulling the chair along with her. "I'm not going to have Anna see me with you in my underwear."

"You've never been the bashful type."

Dropping into her chair, Tri took a deep breath. "Really? The girl who's had a crush on you since we were in school? Who you spend the majority of your time with? Nothing?" Grabbing an unopened bottle of soda, she flung it at him.

Luc ducked it. "What the hell?"

"You're a bad liar. I wish you'd left that girl alone from the start. Not that you'd listen to me. She never did."

Tri flicked the switch that opened the door. "Come on in, hon." She flashed a dirty look at Luc as Anna walked in.

"Hey, sorry Tri. Luc told me to meet him here." Anna had a bag over her shoulder and wore a large olive coloured canvas coat over her sweater. She took a step into the room, wincing. "Wow. It's hot in here."

"Yeah. I like my privacy, as I was telling your idiot friend. Close the door, will ya?"

She did, surveying the room. Luc was still standing in front of the table. "What's going on? You were really cryptic in your message?"

"Yeah," Tri said. "What is going on?"

Luc forced a smile. "I was trying to tell you that and you were biting my head off."

Tri turned to Anna. "I suppose he told you about your brother?"

Anna furrowed her brow. "Yeah. He's… It's a little hard to describe, but he's out for blood, especially for Luc's."

"And he came here, and he had you come here."

"It's okay, really. Dmitri is focused on the slums right now. He promised Luc time to talk to me. He followed through." Anna swallowed hard.

"As far as you know."

"That's fair. I'm pretty sure, though. He was

rather pleased with himself over catching Luc and forcing him to tell me to quit hacking. He actually jumped for joy when I said I would stop."

Tri threw up her hands. "And yet, here you are."

Anna turned to Luc. "Yeah, why am I here, exactly?"

Luc went to the couch and sat. "If we can all calm down for a minute, I can answer both of your questions."

Inhaling sharply, Tri spun her chair to face him. Anna stood where she was, her arms crossed. "Go on."

"Okay." Luc looked from one to the other. "Right. I decoded a message in the broadcast. It's an invitation." He raised an eyebrow.

"Bullshit." Tri folded her arms, mimicking Anna's pose.

"Really?" Anna asked.

Luc nodded. "Yeah."

"So?" Anna took a step towards him.

Luc nodded.

Anna ran over and threw her arms around him. "You better not back out of this one." She let him go and chuckled. "I just got through telling Dmitri I'd take some classes at the Corporate Education Centre." Gritting her teeth, she punched him in the arm.

"Hey!"

"That's for putting me through last night. I was up with Dmitri for hours convincing him that you'd convinced me. I even tried to get him to back off you."

"Ha." Tri snorted out a laugh. "He'd never let Luc off the hook."

"She's right." Luc said.

"I still tried."

Standing, Tri put a foot up on the table. "So, what do you need me for, besides dragging me into Dmitri's line of sight?"

Luc handed her his pocket computer. "For one thing, I need a replacement. Dmitri smashed my good one."

Tri flipped it open. Turning it in her hands, she examined the exterior as she brought it to her desk. She plugged it into a tower and ran a few programs. "Yikes. This is an old octo model. Seen better days too."

"Which is why I need a new one."

Tri looked over her shoulder at him. "How much you willing to spend?"

"Everything. My apartment, everything I can't take with me."

"You're serious about this." Tri straightened.

"Yup."

Tri waved a hand at him. "I've got no interest in your apartment."

"It's a rental anyway."

"There are a few things you have that I can use." She grinned at him as if she knew a secret he didn't.

"I do plan to take a few things with me."

"I want your desktop computer, your Hamm radio—"

"—it doesn't work."

"The parts are worth more than the whole." Luc shrugged.

Tri sat back on her desk. "I want access to your codex and all the program scripts you've written."

"Okay."

"And I want your autographed guitar." Tri raised an eyebrow.

"No problem, but I want the best you have, and none of that crap out front." Luc gestured over his shoulder with a thumb. "And I prefer Mahoney chips if you have any."

Tri furrowed her brow. "But you love that guitar. You turned down a car for that thing."

Luc pressed his lips together. "I can't take it with me."

"You're serious." Tri shifted in place. "You're leaving everything behind?"

"As little as I respect Dmitri for doing what he's done, joining the Consortium, raiding his former friends, and now, tearing down the slums." Luc grimaced. "If anyone can get us all, shut down every hacker in the colony, it's him. He's smart enough and has that damn chip on his shoulder that would drive him all the way back to Earth to take the last of us down."

"And you think there's some kind of salvation out there, in the waste? Where the broadcast comes from?" Tears collected in Tri's eyes, but her face was stern.

"I hope so." Luc pointed to his pocket computer sitting on her desk, still connected. "I believe that message is real. I'm not sure who sent it, but I'm target number one. I'm willing to risk it."

"And Anna?"

Tri and Luc turned to look at the dark-haired woman sitting on the couch, quietly watching them.

Luc smiled at her. "She can make up her own mind." He turned back to Tri. "Besides, it was her idea in the first place."

"You're both crazy."

"Maybe, but there's something else I need from you."

Tri frowned. "What?"

"I don't know where the broadcast comes from."

Twelve
Honest Truth

"Are you kidding me?" Tri grabbed the bottom of her loose shirt and wiped her face. "All that and you don't even know where you're supposed to be going on this big crusade to find the source of the broadcast!"

"I told you. I found the message. That's all I have." Luc went past her and picked up his pocket computer. He brought up the message and handed her the device, the cord connected it to her desktop stretched.

"So? There's all kinds of crap buried in those signals. Half the time it's broken programs or this kind of gibberish," she said.

"You don't have to believe me and I'm not telling you to go. I just need to know the location and you're the most tapped into the Consortium systems that I know." Luc put a hand on her shoulder.

She shrugged it off. "You think if the Consortium knew where the broadcast was coming from they'd just let it continue? I never would have believed you were this stupid, Luc." Thrusting the computer back into his hand, she shoved him. "Stupid and naive." The cable pulled free and dropped to the floor.

Anna stood, but Luc waved her back. "Look, Tri. If you don't know, or even if you do and you don't want to tell me, that's fine. I'll take the computer and find it some other way."

"I don't want your used crap, Luc. I deal in credits."

"Fine." Luc accessed his off-colony bank account and sent her a transfer. "Six thousand. Everything I have. I'll take whatever that can buy me."

The transfer request popped up on one of the screens on her desk.

Anna grabbed his hand from behind and turned him to face her. "Go sit down."

Luc took a deep breath and dropped down onto the spool table. It rocked with his weight. He stared at the monitors, watching the chaos of scrolling code, screen savers, live feeds, and progress bars.

Touching Tri on the back, Anna led her to the far side of the room. Luc struggled to hear them over the fans and found himself leaning forward on his knees. Anna was calm, not moving much. Tri was animated, shaking her head and flailing her arms. After a few minutes they both went back over and sat on the couch.

Clearing his throat, Luc glanced at his watch. It was nearing five in the evening—the small sun would be setting. He rubbed his palms on his legs.

Tri licked her lips and stared at him under cross eyebrows. "I want to know why."

"Why what?" Luc asked.

"You're going. Giving everything up." She looked towards the door to the shop. "Why you risked coming to me when you knew Dmitri was out for blood."

Luc sniffed. "To be honest. Last night I was against it. Even after being put through the ringer. I know Dmitri, what he's about. I know he's going to bring me down one way or another." Scrunching up his face, he wiggled his mouth back and forth. "I know that I probably can't keep myself out of trouble. As soon as I saw the message, I felt like I had to go."

"And?"

"I believe that Dmitri would give me some leeway after I talked to Anna. I thought that I had time to come here before anything happened."

Tri snorted.

Luc set his jaw. "I also knew that he was coming for everyone one way or another and I felt like warning you was the right thing to do. I'd let you know and get the help I need."

"What about her?" Tri nodded towards Anna, who was at the end of the couch, watching them.

"You're going to have to be more specific." Luc scratched an eyebrow.

"Bullshit." Slapping her legs, Tri stood. "You've got to sort yourself out, Luc."

"Fine." Luc stood to face her. "The thought of being separated from Anna sucks. And believe it or not, I agonized over telling her, but as soon as I saw that message. I told her before everything sunk in."

"Finally, some honesty." Tri stepped around him and went over to her desk.

Luc glanced from her to Anna and back. "I've told you the truth about everything from the start of this."

"But you haven't been honest about it." Tri squatted next to a safe under her desk and punched in a code. It swung open with a loud clunk. She reached in and pulled out a sleek box. "I'm still not happy that you ran over here knowing that you were being watched. It's a dick move and you know it. I appreciate the warning, though." She sighed and looked over at Anna. "No offence, but your brother can be an ass."

Anna put up a hand. "Preaching to the choir. I love my brother, but he's done a lot of shit in the last few years."

"Mostly, though, I'm tired of the will-they, won't-they relationship you two have had since we were pimply teenagers." Tri tossed the box to Luc. "Six thousand won't get you an implant, but I don't think that's your style. This is the best pocket model I've got. It's four thousand at my price. I ought to take the six for you putting me through this crap, but for Anna, I'll cut you a break." She reached behind her and accepted the transfer, refunding two thousand credits. "You'll need that since the only thing I know about the location of the broadcast is that it's west of the city. How far or how to get there?" She shrugged.

Luc checked the box. It was a brand new Terra pocket computer. "How did you get your hands on this? It's the latest model."

"I've branched into smuggling since we last talked." Tri smiled and held out her hand. "Okay, that toss was for dramatic effect. I need that back so I can transfer your stuff."

Luc gave her the box and his old computer. She flicked the sleek device open and turned it on—it booted in an instant. She flew through the setup and connected it to her system, copying everything over.

"Thanks, Tri. I'm sorry for coming in hot like that. I was excited and didn't think things through." Luc sat back down. Anna reached over and touched his hand.

"Don't thank me yet. I'm still considering taking that guitar from you." Tri kept her focus on the transfer.

"Go ahead. After this, I'm packing a bag and leaving it all behind."

"What are you going to do to find the place?"

Leaning back, Luc pressed his lips together. "I was thinking about asking Conroy, or maybe even Helmut."

"Damn, you must be serious if you're going to ask Helmut for help." The transfer finished and Tri disconnected the new computer. "What do you want me to do with the old one?"

Luc shrugged. "Still my backup."

Tri stood, scooping up both devices, and crossed the room, handing them to Luc. He took them with a nod.

"Conroy flipped and Helmut would turn you in faster than you can blink. He's been bragging about his plans to take you down for years. The best I can tell you is that the broadcast is coming from somewhere past the mines." Sitting on the table, Tri pointed to Luc's new computer. "I slipped a little something on there for you. Besides some of the maps I've collected, I added a pass to one of the underground raves."

Luc grimaced at her.

"Not my scene either. But if anyone knows where the broadcast comes from, it's either Dolly or Doctor Shadow. One of them will definitely be there tonight."

Luc flicked open the screen. The new device was half as thick as his old one and felt more solid in his hand. The gunmetal grey surface was cool to the touch. It responded as quickly as he could input commands. He brought up the information about the rave and synced his watch.

The invitation glowed green and purple with streaks of pink and blue that shot through the image. It was called the Grave Dance and the picture was of a neon skeleton with swinging joints.

"Did you take my codes?"

"Yeah, and I'll scoop up your desktop and Hamm, too."

Luc looked up at her. "I want you to take the guitar. You're the only other one who would appreciate it all the way out here."

"How about I keep it for you, and when we're both in the mines, we can reminisce together."

Anna stood, prompting Luc to do the same. She hugged Tri, pressing their cheeks together. "Thanks, Triana. You're my favourite."

"Likewise, lady." Tri kissed her forehead as they separated. "No chance I can talk you out of going with him."

Pressing her lips together, Anna shook her head. "Be careful."

"We will."

Luc rubbed his chin. "Thanks, and again, sorry for the trouble."

Tri wrinkled her nose. "It's okay. I know you're a dummy."

Luc stepped over the table. "You know, you could come with us. Keep out of Dmitri's reach."

Crossing her arms, Tri winked at him. "The people I've been working with sneeze with more authority than that loser. Again, no offence, Anna."

"None taken," Anna said, standing by the door.

"I think I'll be okay. For real. I'm mixed up with some heavy hitters in the local government and with the Consortium off world. When I go down, it'll be their doing, not Dmitri's."

Luc smiled at her and nodded. "I'll leave my key in the place where we hide things."

"I remember."

Thirteen
CreeperKings

Luc and Anna headed back to his apartment. The waning sun dipped over the wall on the far side of the city. Light from lampposts and what little spilled out from still open businesses did its best to make up for the loss. People returning home from work filled the street, heading out to take care of errands, or finding some relaxation after a long day. Cars waited in long lines at streetlights and stop signs, eager commuters honking.

Anna kept close to Luc, her teeth chattering as the temperature plummeted. "You know, sometimes this colony is pretty nice." She leaned into him and Luc put an arm around her. "It's almost normal if you let yourself get caught up in the day-to-day stuff."

Luc watched the people going about their business, some cheery, some miserable. Normal was right. The snippets of lives he saw were unremarkable, but appealing.

He half-smiled. "It reminds me of what I can remember of Earth."

"How old were you when you came to TRAPPIST?" Anna stuck her arm into his open jacket and around his waist.

"Ten, eleven. Telbak still ran the colony. No one believed the Consortium was real."

"And this is what Earth was like?" She squeezed him. "It's not bad. A little cold."

The half-smile expanded across Luc's face. "Haha." He scanned the scene, spotted a few bars in close proximity on the opposite side of the street. People were spilling out of them, congregating together into a jumble. Luc pointed to the mass. "It was like that. A lot of people everywhere, all the time. Dirty streets—constantly loud. There were so many neat things to see. There was a place my dad used to talk about, the Wall. Not like the city wall. It was a place, a colony in the middle of the big city that burrowed into the ground like the mines, but it was all one thing. It was supposed to be filled with monsters and things that used to be people. Even more so than the city itself."

They kept walking, leaving the main road behind. "It's all a blur by now, but at times, this place feels similar."

The few people who had been walking or driving along the house-lined side streets disappeared. The sound of activity behind them converted into a flock-of-birds incoherence. Luc spotted a purple and yellow face painted on the side of a nearby building.

"Shit. I meant to cut around this neighbourhood." Luc let go of Anna and she did the same. He took her hand and started to hurry down the sidewalk.

"What?" Anna tried to look everywhere, her head swivelling back and forth.

"It's CreeperKings territory. They took the whole block. It was tense enough coming through it in the middle of the afternoon. We're prime targets walking like this."

"Should we run?"

Luc grimaced and huffed. "I don't want to draw more attention if we don't have to."

The sound of shattering glass echoed down a nearby alleyway followed by a whoop and clumping feet.

"Okay, run."

Luc took off, pulling Anna along with him. As soon as he did, more hoots and shouts came from behind them. Like a dog seeing something to chase, the CreeperKing street thugs started their hunt.

Their breath collected into clouds that swirled as they ran, dissipating into wisps under the streetlights. Luc tried to estimate how many blocks they had to get through before they were out of the Kings' territory, then he tried to convince himself the gang would stop as soon as he and Anna were past the imaginary line.

Anna had let go of his hand and was running beside him. "Got a plan?" Her nose was red and the words came out stiff.

"Not…yet." Luc struggled to keep his breath. He glanced behind them and saw the gang less than a block behind. They ran in a group, bouncing and weaving around each other, giving their victims a chance to stay ahead. He caught glimpses of purple jackets with yellow symbols on them and spiked hair. He also saw the wooden planks, bottles, and pipes they carried as well as the glint of light reflecting off more than one knife.

"They're…playing…with…us."

Anna darted down an alley, tugging on Luc's jacket, pulling him with her. She ducked under a broken wooden fence and he followed, dropping onto his stomach to fit through the gap. They slowed their pace, trying to keep the noise down. Luc heard the group stop at the mouth of the alley.

"You want to make it a game, Nor-man, Nor-ma?" one of the Kings shouted, the others laughing and cheering. "We like games! We win at games!"

Anna led Luc around the house that was behind

the fence, and to the front yard. "Norma?" she whispered.

"Slang for normals." Luc managed between breaths.

She nodded and crouched behind a half-dead bush.

"We can't hide. They'll find us sooner or later," he said.

Keeping her focus on the street, Anna pulled a branch out of her line of sight. "I'm just watching. I thought I noticed something about them while they were chasing us."

"Okay." Luc went to the fence on their left that separated the first property of the block from the next. He peered through a gap in the boards and saw two of the gang members searching the yard and peeking into the house. He went back to Anna and tapped her on the shoulder, pointing towards them. When she looked, he held up two fingers.

She nodded to the street corner as four more goons passed a streetlight. They heard a crunching behind them and turned in time to see another King, yellow bobbles hanging from a torn purple leather jacket, slink around the corner.

"Got you," he said.

Luc saw his teeth as the man smiled. They were all gold, glinting in the faint light. He also noticed a shine covering his eyes, but the man yelled before

Luc could figure out why.

"Here they are! I caught them. I get first dibs!" The King jumped to his feet and swung a bat over his head.

"Not caught yet," a woman said, lunging through the bushes, grabbing at Anna.

Luc sprung to his feet and pulled Anna back as she kicked the woman in the face.

The King squealed and fell to the ground, holding her nose. "That dirty Norma is mine!"

Gold-teeth wrapped his bat over Luc's shoulders and pulled him off his feet. "I called it, I found them!"

Luc jammed his head back and Anna grabbed the man around the legs. They managed to topple him, breaking his grip. The two Kings in the adjacent yard clambered over the fence and the ones on the street charged.

Anna jumped over the downed thug and ran for the alley. "Come on!"

Luc followed, taking a moment to kick the fence, knocking one of the thugs from it. Diving to his stomach, he followed Anna through the hole in the wood and back to the street.

"They're wearing goggles," she said, leading him towards his neighbourhood.

"What?" Luc thought of the shine over gold-teeth's eyes.

"All of them that I saw. Goggles."

"So?" Luc furrowed his brow but got to the answer before Anna could tell him. "I got it." He reached into his jacket and pulled out his new computer. Keeping Anna in his periphery, he logged into the device and found a network access point. It was locked behind a protocol with the Rancore Siblings signature at the top of the page. Luc ran one of his old backdoor programs, but it failed. He checked what code he could from the page and found a mistake. His thumbs flying across the keys, he altered his program and ran it again. The wall fell and he had access to the Sibling's systems.

Anna changed directions and pulled on his arm, moving him out of the way of a pole. "Hurry, they're on us."

Luc noticed the sound of them. They weren't hooting, they were almost growling. He risked a glance and saw them a few houses back, sprinting in a pack, the thrill of the chase replaced with anger.

Focusing back on the screen, Luc found the system running tech for the CreeperKings. A message popped up on over the image.

Think you're bad? You're going to wish you were dead messing with our network. A warning flashed in the corner, letting him know he was being hacked.

Sneering through his deep breaths, he risked a reply. *I'm going to pay you two back for letting your goons chase me. You still owe me for warning you about the raid last year.* Luc dipped into his vault and found a nasty virus he'd saved from an attack one of the other corporations ran on the Consortium years back. It was buried deep in one of the broadcasts, and he had kept it for himself.

The warning disappeared and the file structure on the Rancore system started to vanish. Luc managed to get into the controls for the goggles the CreeperKings were wearing and amped up the brightness.

All the gang members chasing them screamed. Luc stopped running and looked back. They were on the ground, stripping the goggles from their eyes.

Another message appeared on his screen. *Luc, we're sorry. We didn't know it was you. Please don't—* It cut off as the virus ate that part of their system.

"Good job." Anna leaned against him, huffing.

"You too." Luc pulled up his antivirus software and ran it on the Rancore network. "That was all you. Good idea with the goggles."

"Thanks. We should go."

Luc nodded and closed his computer.

Fourteen
Plans Made

Luc slammed open the door to his apartment. Anna dropped her bag on the table and sat on the end of his bed.

"That was close. And it's just the beginning." Luc went over to his desk and plugged in the new computer. It was way faster than his desktop, but he still needed to finish setting it up and transfer all his network data and controls over to it.

"This city is getting worse and worse." Anna flopped onto her back. "I can't believe the Rancore siblings have stooped to working with that nut-job street gang."

"All the more reason to leave it behind." Letting the computers do their work, Luc went to his closet and pulled out a backpack. It was old, with fraying seams reinforced with safety pins and a finicky zipper. The waxed canvas was worn and soft in some spots, but it was sturdy enough.

Grabbing clothes, he alternated stuffing them in the bag and tossing them over his shoulder. With a couple of extra t-shirts, a sweater and a second pair of pants, along with assorted underwear and socks, he left his closet and went back to the desk. From a drawer, he grabbed a battery pack and charging cables, a case filled with microdisks, a tool roll, and a parts bag.

He turned to Anna as he shifted the contents to fit better. "Check the kitchen. See if there's something we can take with us. We have no way to know how long we'll be in the wastes." Slipping off the jacket, he pulled on the hoodie that he had left to dry. It was a little stiff, but comfortable. He put his jacket back on and reached behind his head to free the hood from under the synthetic leather.

Anna got to her feet and flung open cabinets and the small refrigerator. "There's not much. A few supplement bars."

"We'll have to pick something up." Luc stopped and pointed at her. "Can you take care of that? I have to get to the Grave Dance and see if Dolly or Shadow know anything."

"Dolly hates you for distributing all those educational programs a few years back. That was the corner of her business." Anna crossed her arms.

"And Shadow is a psychopath." Luc nodded.

"I think it's sociopath."

Luc pressed his lips together. "It's all or nothing at this point. Dolly is reasonable enough. I can offer her my decoding software. She'll trade. As for Shadow—"

"Hope Dolly has the location?"

"Yup." Luc zipped up the bag, pulling the slider back to make sure the teeth closed.

"There are a few things I can get while you're gone, even though I think it's stupid to go on your own." Anna shut the cupboards and leaned on the counter.

Luc scratched his head. "Probably, but it'll be easier to get in and around on my own. Those raves are designed to be disorienting. Besides, as soon as your brother figures out what's going on, he's going to lose his shit."

"Yeah. He was pretty suspicious when I left earlier. I had to drop my bag into the bushes from the balcony." Anna mimicked the fall with her hand. "By now, he may have people out looking for us."

"Better to split up, then." Throwing the bag over his shoulder, Luc disconnected his new pocket computer and stuck it into an inner jacket pocket. He unplugged his desktop computer and set it on top of the Hamm radio then pulled the guitar off his wall, leaning against the end of the desk. Going back to the middle section he slid out a yellow and black striped box. He flipped open the lid to reveal a red button. "Here goes everything." Slamming his fist down, the network servers under the desk started to smoke and fizzle. "What the virus doesn't get, the overload should take care of."

Luc sighed, watching the sparks flash inside the cases and the thin lines of smoke curling away from them.

Anna slipped beside him and hugged his arm. "You going to be okay?"

Nodding, Luc rubbed his eyes. "Yeah. Just a lot of work went into that. Most of it is on the new one." He tapped his chest where the pocket computer was. "It just feels very final."

"I get it. We have lives here. Leaving them behind is difficult, even if it's exciting. Even if things here aren't so good."

Luc looked down at her. "They weren't all bad."

Anna shook her head, still watching the destruction. "No. But they're about to change—for the worse." Letting go, she slapped her hands together. "Nothing to do about it now. We'd better get moving before we run out of time."

"Yeah. Let's meet back here when we're done. If it's not safe, we should meet at the diner. Hopefully the fact that it'll be full of people should keep any soldiers civil."

Anna raised an eyebrow at him.

"I know. Not likely. Still."

"Third option, we should meet near the mine exit. Somewhere close to the checkpoint," Anna said.

Luc nodded. "Good idea. Do me a favour and buy me some gloves?"

"I'll add it to the list." Taking out her own pocket computer, she started to type. "Anything else?"

"If I think of anything, I'll send you a message, but I'll put it in the network chat. We should still have access to everything that was in the cloud. It's pretty secure. I never put anything sensitive on the public systems and even with the Consortium code monkeys on his side, it should take Dmitri a while to get in."

Anna snapped her computer shut and grabbed her backpack. "Got any style in mind, for the gloves?" She smiled and Luc snorted a laugh.

"I'll trust that to you. Keep your head down and your ears open."

"Yeah. You too."

Luc slipped on his own backpack, took a long look at his apartment, and headed for the door. Before he opened it, Anna wrapped her arms around him.

"Be safe. I'm starting to get nervous."

Luc hugged her back. "I know the feeling. I'll try to be quick."

They separated and Luc opened the door. Anna

left as he locked it. Taking out his computer, he set up an automatic transfer to send his landlord the next month's rent, with a little extra for having to clear the place out for him. Slipping his computer back into his jacket, he headed outside.

He stopped on the front stoop and crouched as if he were tying his shoe. Pulling out a loose brick from where the wall met the floor, he stuck his keys in the open space behind it and slid the brick back as quickly as he could.

The sun was gone and the moon, with its smaller hangers on, was crawling low across the sky.

Standing, Luc zipped his jacket and hitched up his bag. A fine rain was misting, slicking the street. He clomped down the steps to his building and headed downtown.

Fifteen
Hidden Markers

The closer Luc got to the downtown core, the brighter the city became. Unlike the yellowed and inconsistent streetlights of the neighbourhoods, the city centre was lit in bright white, subtle blues, and the occasional neon rainbow from signs that hung over the streets. People in suits and fine dresses glided down the clean sidewalks, popping in and out of boutiques, restaurants, and high-end social clubs. Luc felt conspicuous and kept his head low and his hood up. There were other people like him. Lower class citizens on errands—often for one of the wealthy Consortium employees hobnobbing around them—or on some other job that required them to venture into the nicer part of the colony.

Luc risked the occasional glance at the passers-by, and relaxed when he noticed they were avoiding looking at him, too. He cut down an alley as soon as he was deep enough downtown to stay off the main streets. The alleys were a maze-like network of corridors, short tunnels, and bridges that wove around, under, and through the large buildings in the core.

Stopping behind a theatre on the main floor of an office building, Luc searched for one of the hobo-markers that acted as signposts through the maze. He'd been part of constructing the routes when he was first getting into the hacking scene, but after years of others taking over, he had forgotten how to manoeuvre through the labyrinth.

Under a layer of scribbled graffiti, he found a line with three hatches running across it. It was the symbol they used to mark the start of a path. He traced it with a finger and found the angular face sitting on its side that marked the direction.

Hoping he remembered correctly, he started to jog towards a bridge that led over a side street and felt his watch vibrate. Glancing down, he saw a message scroll across the little screen under the dials.

Luc. Been monitoring the chatter on the military frequency. Dmitri has sent out a warrant for you and Anna. I let her know too. Expect trouble. I'm burning our connection. Good luck – T.

Nodding to himself, Luc thanked Tri in his head and climbed up the steps to the pedestrian bridge.

"Okay. I'm on a timetable now and I have security officers and probably some off-duty soldiers on the lookout for me." He huffed. "Keep to the plan."

A Consortium patrol car drove under the bridge and Luc tensed. He forced himself to keep walking even though he was sure it had slowed down.

"They don't know where you are," he mumbled.

Descending the stairs back into the alleys, he scanned the walls for the next marker. He knew that the raves rotated locations regularly, but there were only so many places that could hold parties that big. The clue on the invitation was the skeleton, he hoped. Usually anything to do with bones meant the original landing site of the Telbak colony ship. It was used as the first building and the rest of the city was built around it. As the city grew, the centre of power shifted and the landing site with its old, warehouse-like buildings, was left as a storage site.

Luc remembered actually getting a tour of the colony ship while still in a Telbak-run school. It was the old computer systems that sparked his interest in coding. He imagined creating the programs that would run such a behemoth as it blasted through space faster than light.

Clenching his teeth, Luc pushed the thought away and found the next marker. It was a rudimentary drawing of the colony ship as a skeletal animal. The position of the planets around it pointed him north, through an underpass. He ended up at a series of connected alleys with multiple junctions and dead ends.

The sound of a siren reverberated into the maze from a nearby street. Luc jumped behind a garbage bin and waited for the sound to pass. He picked up his pace and crossed under another street into a courtyard behind one of the corporate offices. Staying in the shadows of the tunnel, he scanned the windows and glass doors for security. Light shone through them, casting shadows and competing with the overhead lights mounted on a pole in the middle of the square. He thought he could see a shadow move back and forth, patrolling the courtyard, but he couldn't tell if it was outside or inside the lobby of the building.

He sniffed and charged forward, walking deliberately towards the adjacent tunnel that went through the building to his left. As soon as he was in the light someone came out of the glass door.

"Hey, you. Stop."

Luc kept walking, angling away from the voice.

"I said stop. This is Consortium property and off limits to you."

Luc bit his lip and walked faster. The whole colony was Consortium property, technically, but he didn't think correcting the guard would do him any good.

"I said stop." He grabbed Luc by the shoulder.

Luc pulled down his hood, pretending to pull his

headphones off as well. "Huh?" He glanced at the guard out of the corner of his eye, trying not to face him head on. "Oh, sorry, I had my music too loud. What was that?" Luc's mouth felt dry.

"What music? I don't hear nothing?" The man spun Luc to face him.

Grimacing, Luc pulled out his micro-disc player. "I stopped it."

The man scrunched his face. "Yeah, right. You got some identification?"

Luc stuffed his player in a pocket and dug inside his jacket. "Yeah, here somewhere. What's this about? I'm just passing through."

"Passing through a back alley, at night? In this part of town? Where you going?"

"I was on a repair job and just finished. I'm in IT, private contractor." Luc patted his jacket and stuck his hand into another pocket. "I know I have my ID somewhere."

"Where were you working?" The guard shifted his weight to the side, his hand on his belt.

"It was, uh, the shipping offices, off of Fourth and Terminal Street. The main offices, not the actual receiving, obviously."

"Uh huh." The guard looked over Luc's shoulder as if he were trying to remember where the shipping office was. "You got anything to prove you were on the job?"

"Yeah." Luc swung his backpack off his shoulder and dug out his bag of parts and tool roll. "Tools of the trade."

The guard shone a light down on them. "And why're there clothes in the bag? Planning on going somewhere?"

"I'm staying at a friend's place. He lives closer to work, so late-night jobs like this, he lets me crash on his couch." Luc stuffed his tools and parts back in the bag and pulled the zipper closed, his fingers slipping several times.

"Looks like you need a new backpack." There was a chirp on the guard's radio. He checked the monitor strapped to the inside of his wrist and pressed the button on the receiver by his shoulder. "Yeah?"

Standing, Luc tensed—ready to run.

"Hold on, I've got some IT guy back here." The guard looked up from his monitor. "Get out of here, and you should take the streets to your friend's house next time."

"Thank you, sir. I'll make sure to do that." Luc turned and walked away. He counted his steps, making sure he wasn't going too quickly, though he was sure he looked stiff and weird.

"What was that?" The guard said, looking at his monitor again.

Luc made it to the end of the tunnel through the

building and ran. He took the first turn he came to and kept changing directions, putting as much distance between himself and the guard as he could.

Broadcast Wasteland

Sixteen
Snowdrifts

Luc came out of a tunnel and saw the original colony ship. The top fin peeked over the large, squat buildings that surrounded it. There were no lights on in the warehouse district, but he could hear the faint thumping of music coming from behind the massive spaceship.

Feeling his way through the canyon like pathways, he listened for the sound. The moons were high, casting dim light and deep shadows. Luc walked around a corner, the sound getting louder, and felt the music through the wall of the building he was using as a guide. He circled around to the front and spotted two people guarding a door. A tall, thin man with a shaved head and an all black leather outfit leaned against the wall. Next to him was a plump woman dancing to the beats that escaped through the closed door behind her.

The man spotted Luc, his left eye glowing with the tell-tale sign of an implant. Luc figured that selling implants was how Tri got the invitation in the first place.

"Hey, old man. You better run along before you get yourself into trouble." The man crossed his hands in front of his crotch and kinked his neck.

The woman chortled. "Yeah, old man. Nothing here for you." She caressed her figure and laughed again.

Luc walked up to them, already tired of the shtick. He could feel his eyelids sitting low as he took out his computer and beamed the invitation to the bouncers.

"So, you think you're hard? This place is going to eat you alive." The man sneered as he opened the door. "Don't say I didn't warn you."

The woman smiled and looked like she was about to laugh again, but froze when Luc passed her.

As Luc went through the doorway he could hear her whisper his name to the bouncer.

The door shut, leaving Luc in a dark hallway. At the far end, he could see the bleeding of flashing lights leak through a curtain that blocked off the rest of the building. The sound, louder inside the building, was muted by the thick fabric. He checked his watch. It had taken him forty minutes to get to the rave, and he was certain the woman at the door knew something about security looking for him. Hurrying, he headed for the end of the hallway, but saw a bright, white light cut through the wall to his left.

At first, he thought it was a door. The point of light slid from the floor to just over his head and moved across before dropping back to the floor. He took a step back and realized that it appeared on an exterior wall. The impossible door swung inward and swirling snow drifted into the dark hallway, buffeting the opposite wall and falling into a heap. With the snow came a breeze even colder than the plummeting nights in the colony.

A hooded figure peeked through the open doorway, looking in both directions. He paused when he saw Luc.

"Is this Earth?" The voice from the figure was higher pitched than Luc would have guessed and caught him off guard.

"No." Luc swallowed. "This is TRAPPIST colony."

The figure grunted, shaking his head. "Sorry to bother you."

He started to withdraw, but Luc rushed forward, his hand outstretched. "Wait! I need help."

"So do I."

"Maybe, uh, we can help each other." Luc looked down at his hands.

"I don't think I can help you."

Luc stepped forward again but stopped when the figure started to retreat through the doorway. "I need to know where the broadcast comes from."

"I don't know what that is."

"What do you need help with?" Luc blurted out the words without thinking. The figure reminded him of a boy he knew in school. Kind, but timid. Shy, until approached.

"I'm trying to find my way home. I don't think you can help me."

Luc shook his head. "Good luck."

"Yeah." The figure backed through the doorway and the section of wall closed behind him. A last puff of snow squeaked through the crack. "You too."

When the door closed, the light vanished. Luc stared at the spot. The curtain at the end of the hallway opened, letting in laser light and booming sound. A woman stumbled towards him and stopped when she saw the snow.

With effort, she looked up at Luc. "That snow?"

"I think so." Luc squinted. She brought the smell of the rave. Sweat, smoke, and booze.

"You do that?" She pointed at him and nearly fell, clinging to the wall for support.

Luc shook his head as she dropped to her knees and stuck her hand in the small pile.

"That's snow, dude. Like, real snow. How'd you

do that?" Twiddling her fingers, the snow fell through them, back to the pile.

"I didn't." Luc walked past her and pushed through the curtain.

The sound hit him like a wall. He winced and covered his ears. The entire warehouse was full of people including a second level that sat like a balcony spanning half of the building. There were even people on catwalks.

Tight beams of green, purple, yellow, and red flashed from fixtures hanging from the ceiling and walls. A cloud of smoke hovered over the main floor—a mix of narcotics, vapour from the dancers, and synthetic smoke shooting from jets set about the room. The DJ was on a spinning platform floating halfway between the floor and the balcony. Immediately to the left of the door was a counter. A man wearing glowing makeup leaned over it and yelled at Luc.

"Take your coat and bag? One credit each."

Luc shook his head and pushed into the crowd, swinging his bag into his arms. He was jostled from all directions and felt warm, slick skin stick to him. Holding his breath, he forced his way to the bar at the far side of the dance floor. Dozens of people were clamouring to get the servers' attention, each claiming they knew someone more important than the others.

Luc stood off to the side, a coin in his fingers. A bartender with a half-shaved head and a nearly sheer, sleeveless top came up to him.

"What can I get you, hun?" she yelled over the music and clamour.

Luc slipped the coin to her and leaned closer. "I'm looking for Dolly or Doctor Shadow."

She started to walk away, but Luc shifted positions to stay in front of her. "Just tell whichever one is here that Luc is looking for them."

Snatching up the coin, she moved to another customer.

Luc turned and watched the chaos happening in front of him. He remembered going to raves when he was just out of school, but the ones he went to were half as big, and half as crazy.

Sweat flew out from the scantily clad dancers as they gyrated and flung themselves around with abandon. Luc took a step closer to the wall to avoid the spray coming off of a girl who was whipping her wet hair around like a windmill. The bartender slid a drink in front of him.

"Complements of a friend of yours." She nodded to the far end of the long bar. Through the crowd, he spotted flowing rainbow coloured hair obscuring the face of a woman just tall enough to lean on the bar.

Luc placed another coin down and the bartender

made it disappear before she turned to help another patron.

Picking up the glass, Luc sniffed the drink. The pale green liquid smelled mostly sweet with a sour tang that hung in his nostrils. He took a sip and his mouth puckered. Holding the drink close to his chest, he manoeuvred to the opposite end of the bar, trying to keep the rainbow haired woman in sight.

She turned and started to walk away by the time he was halfway to her. People parted for her, almost as an instinct.

Luc put his drink down and used the free hand to push and pull his way forward.

She climbed up a set of stairs to a closed off area that looked like it had been the warehouse office at one time. A large woman, a head taller and half-again as broad as Luc, moved aside for the woman, but put her hand out to block him.

"I'm following that woman," Luc said, trying to look around the bulk of the bouncer.

"Lots of people follow her." The woman looked over Luc, as if he were an annoyance and the real threat was somewhere behind him.

"I know her. She bought me a drink. I came here specifically to see her."

"You and half the jokers here, bud." The bouncer gave him a little shove and Luc stumbled back, colliding with a large tattooed man who was dancing at the edge of the crowd.

Luc grabbed hold of the railing to pull himself upright and spun, ready to defend himself, but the guy helped him up and offered a bottle of water. Shaking his head, Luc went back to the bouncer.

"Just tell Dolly that I'm sorry the way things went down—"

"I ain't no messenger, pal." The woman touched the earpiece she was wearing and stepped to the side of the stairs. "You can go in." Her tone hadn't changed, and she still looked past him as if he were barely there.

"Thanks." Luc had to step around her to get by and she bumped him against the railing as he passed.

Seventeen
Dolly

The interior of the former office turned VIP area was brightly lit and the air was clear. The sound of the party raging on the other side of the door was muted and mostly drowned out by the hum of a ventilation system working on overdrive. There were some couches, a private bar, and a projected view of the club on three of the walls. The fourth wall was made of tinted windows from the floor to the ceiling with a single steel door. Luc could make out a second lounge and what looked like an office through the opaque glass.

He tried the inner door, but it was locked. Hearing a click from an overhead speaker, he remembered the ordeal he had to go through with Tri.

"Hey there, Luc." The voice over the speaker was high-pitched and peppy. "I'm absolutely shocked to see you, especially at one of my parties."

"Dolly." Luc forced a smile. "It's been a while."

"Has it? I wouldn't know. I all but forgot about you a long time ago, buckaroo."

Taking a deep breath, Luc scrunched up his face. "Uh, about that."

"Water under the bridge, cowboy. I'm not the same nervous, starry-eyed girl that I was a decade ago. I'm a success. I'm someone important in the underground on this colony. You, on the other hand, are a bum who still runs around hacking radio towers so he can eke out a living selling copies of the broadcast."

Luc shrugged. "You got me pegged there. I need a favour."

"I know exactly what you need, Luc. And that's not me being cute. I've been keeping an eye on you and your little quest. I know what Dmitri is up to and I could tell you where your little Anna is right now."

Luc went over to the nearest couch and sat on the back of it. "I thought you forgot about me."

"Let's not play games, buddy-boy. I'm just about good and over our little spat, but I'm not stupid. I keep an eye on troublemakers—Dmitri being a big source of trouble for people like me. I make it a point to know what he knows, and he has an unhealthy obsession with you."

"Thanks for clarifying. If you know why I'm

here, can we cut to the chase?"

The tint on the window faded away and Dolly was standing on the opposite side. She was short, her long hair reaching to her knees. Standing with her arms crossed, she tilted her head to the side. "I'm currently debating that with Shadow."

Luc scanned the room behind Dolly. There were several workstations that made Tri's back office look quaint. A large table in the middle of the room was covered in piles of papers, discs, credits, and bags of various sizes. An overhead projector displayed an image on the table that he couldn't make out.

"I don't see him here. He out on the floor, or at some secondary location?"

Dolly frowned. "We have our hands in quite a few different pots." She tapped the side of her head. "He's watching this, though. You could say hi, but he's less happy to see you than I am."

Luc dropped his bag at his feet. "I know why you don't like me—and to be honest, I don't blame you. In fact, undercutting your market is one of my big regrets."

Dolly let her arms drop. "Let's just chalk that up to the stupidity of youth."

Luc nodded. "You're doing me a kindness to say so. What I don't get is what he has against me."

"It's not what he has against you. It's just good business. You're a liability even without Dmitri worming his way into his new position—or his general fury towards you. You're content with so little when you could have done so much. You taught us all everything you knew when we got started. Now we've all left you in the dust."

Luc shrugged. "Nothing to argue with, there."

Dolly giggled. "Though, you did do a number on the Rancore Siblings. That was a cute little move, but a bit overkill, don't ya think"

"The street gang they teamed up with was literally chasing me at the time. I have little sympathy for them."

Running her hand through her multi-coloured hair, Dolly sighed. "People in the game are getting more and more desperate. It was nice to see you still had something up your sleeve. Shadow sees you as a threat." She frowned. "He wants to turn you in, try to get some immunity in the bargain."

Dolly took another step towards the glass. "I think you're more trustworthy than Dmitri. And, maybe, a bit more stable."

"Trustworthy, sure. Stable?" Luc put his hand out and wobbled it. "I'm just offering you a deal."

Dolly snickered. "I'm not interested in obsolete viruses from the stone age."

"Seemed to do the trick just fine. But that's not what I'm offering." Taking out his computer, Luc flipped open the lid.

Dolly jumped back. "What are you doing?"

"Relax." Luc went up to the window so she could see the small screen.

"Where'd you get that piece of tech? It's pretty slick for an external device." Dolly put a hand on the glass and leaned closer to the computer.

His thumbs punching in commands, Luc kept his inputs fast enough to prevent Dolly from tracking them. "Tri. Cost me my life savings, but it's more important to me now than credits."

Her eyes flitting to his bag, Dolly straightened. "You're running."

"Yup. But I need you to tell me where." Luc focused on the screen.

"I don't have any access to ships or shuttles. Tri's the one to talk to about that."

"Not my play. You got a server I can download something to?"

"What have you dug up, RadDude?"

Luc looked over his shoulder at her. "Et tu, Brute?"

Dolly winked. "Cough it up."

Sighing, Luc turned to face her. "I found a message in the broadcast. It's an invitation."

"And you need to know where it's coming from. Didn't find that hidden in the code?"

Luc shook his head. "I'm having a fire sale. Gave Tri my codex and scripts."

"Who says I know the location?" Dolly put her hands on her hips.

"You want in on this or not?"

Looking up and away, Dolly focused on something that Luc couldn't see. He guessed it was the image her implant was projecting.

"Shadow is threatening to call security on you if I don't do it myself."

"Tell Shadow he's a short sighted, scaredy-cat and at best a moron." Luc looked around the lounge and walked over to the bar. He checked the small fridge behind it and took a can of cold coffee. "You mind?"

"He can see and hear you."

Luc stuck up his middle finger and spun in place. "He see that?"

Dolly sighed. "Why can you never play nice?"

"I was trying." Taking the can with him, Luc went back to the window. "I'm surprised security isn't here already. I haven't been terribly subtle today. You want to make a deal or not?"

The lights in the room dimmed and a series of warnings popped up on the screens on both sides of the glass. Security forces were closing in.

Dolly ran to the closest terminal and brought up a security feed and reports coming in from her staff. "Now you did it, Luc. You had to open your big mouth."

Eighteen
Raid

Luc took another sip of the coffee. "I still may have something you want. You up for that trade now, or should I start running and we can both come away with nothing for our troubles?"

"You screwed me over, Luc." Dolly left the computer behind and stomped to the window. "We were friends."

Luc grimaced. "It was the right thing to do."

She hit the glass with her palm. "Screw the right thing. You've always thought you knew what that was—always thought you were better than the rest of us."

"Not better." Shaking his head, Luc made a fist and rapped a knuckle on the window frame. "I know I cut your business out from under you by distributing the educational software and books, but I tried to bring you in on my work."

"I never wanted to fight for scraps, obsessed over a radio broadcast, one step ahead of the Consortium. You decided for me."

"Let me make it up to you." Luc held up his pocket computer.

There was a knock on the door. "Hey, boss. What are we doing about security?"

Luc saw Dolly check her personal projection. "Shit. I'm calling it." Hurrying over to the terminal, she executed a code on the machine. The music stopped and someone screamed. A recorded announcement told everyone to evacuate and to take the back exits in order to avoid Consortium guards.

"Thanks for burning me again." She stared at him, her lip curled.

"Like I said. Let me make it up to you."

Dolly rushed for the door and slammed it open. She walked up to Luc and shoved him. He staggered back, stopping himself before backing into the couch. "For shit's sake. What do you have that can make up for this? You can't even pay me back for screwing me over years ago."

"I'm trying to give you my decoding programs." Luc meandered back to Dolly. She looked up at him, blinking.

Luc brought his pocket computer back up. "So? Where am I sending this? Or would you prefer discs?" He took a disc out of his jacket and slipped it into the machine.

"You're an asshole." Dolly sighed and went back through the door.

After a moment, Luc picked up his backpack and followed. "What does that mean?"

Dolly had grabbed a bag and was filling it with the papers and credits on the table. "You mess with people. You play mind games."

"This is no game. I'm trying to find out where the broadcast is coming from and I'm willing to give up just about anything to get it."

Stopping in mid scoop, Dolly looked up at him. "And is Anna coming with you?"

"Yeah." Luc clenched his jaw. "Is that what this is about? You're worried about her?"

"No, you idiot. It's about the chaos you cause with no care for anyone but yourself." Dolly threw down the pile of credits she was holding. The coins, worth more than Luc had ever earned, scattered across the table and onto the floor. "You're a hurricane that draws people in and destroys them. I had to start from scratch, and now you're here and you're doing it all over again."

Luc scrunched up his face. "I'm sorry. I guess I'm more self-centred than I realized."

"That doesn't fix anything, Luc."

"You're right. What can I do?"

Dolly went back to filling her bag. "Too late now.

You're leaving and one of my very expensive and difficult to build clubs is being raided." She nodded to the screen across the table. Consortium guards were swarming the warehouse, grabbing everyone they could. Most of the huge crowd was still managing to slip away in the bedlam.

"I can still give you the software." Luc ejected the freshly copied disc and held it out to her.

Sneering at him, she snatched it and tucked it into her bra. "I'm still pissed at you."

"That's fair. I'm sorry for bringing the Consortium to your club."

Dolly heaved the bag onto the table. "Shit, Luc. We get raided every other week. It's not that big a city. This one is probably on you, though." Walking over to the terminal, she held her hand out. "Computer, please."

Luc placed his pocket computer into her hand and she connected it to a cable on the desk.

"Not worried about viruses?"

"Please. I've got software from the corporations that won't even run on most of the computers on this colony. While you were out playing Robin Hood, the rest of us were busy." She compressed a file and sent it across to his device.

"And what about me? Not going to just take all my stuff."

"I've got what I want." Dolly tapped the disc

under her shirt. "Been wanting this for a long time. It's the one thing you did better than the rest of us."

The file finished transferring and Luc's watch buzzed. Dolly unplugged the pocket computer and held it out while she punched in a series of shortcuts that started a rapid wipe of the local system.

"So, what did I get there?"

Dolly put a hand on her hip. "Coordinates, smart guy. I don't have an exact location, but I know the general area."

"How general?"

Frowning, Dolly put her hands out and moved them apart, stopped, then expanded the distance.

"What does that mean?"

"It's an approximation. You'll see." Dolly went back to the table. "I've got access to the satellites, or, I did."

"Did?"

Dolly crossed her arms. "I do, but the network keeps dropping out. Started a couple days ago. The satellites have moved positions, too. I can still connect, but it's…intermittent."

"That's still kind of handy. I suppose you have a back way out of here?" Luc asked.

Dolly sighed and stared at him. "Fine, you carry the bag—but I'm doing this for Anna."

Luc swung his backpack over his shoulder as Dolly stuffed her pockets with as many of the remaining credits as she could. She hurried over to a door along the back wall, coins clattering to the floor as she ran. Luc grabbed the bag from the table and had to stop.

"Damn. How'd you lift this thing?" He grunted and scooped it into both of his arms, the handles poking him in the face.

"I'm not a million years old." Opening the door, Dolly paused to look up at the personal image that her implant projected. "Wilhelm, I'm running, get out of there." She glanced back at Luc who brought his knee up to steady the full bag. "The bouncer outside my door. She's a good employee."

Luc clenched his teeth. "Great story. Can we go?"

"Fine." Dolly rolled her eyes and led him down a dark hallway. There were doors marked as bathrooms and one as a utility closet. Beyond them, at the end of the hall, was a large poster of the colony from the early days when Telbak was advertising it as a destination with opportunity.

Dolly ran her hand down the outside frame and a small, nearly invisible hatch opened next to it. She leaned in and a scanner read her retina with a red and green glow, like at the checkpoints. When the scan was finished, the poster swung inward with a click. Dolly winked at Luc and stepped over the threshold into a smaller hallway that looked like it was from the original construction of the warehouse. When they were both through, she closed the panel.

"This leads down to a tunnel that connects to all the other buildings around here. Shadow and I blocked most of them off." Dolly made an explosion sound and mimicked the blast with her hands. "Totally imploded them. Then we reinforced the ones we wanted, covering them in RF blocking foil. We even built some stuff over them to look like the old buildings. They're as secure as something can be on the colony."

"Impressive." Luc shifted his grip on the bag, straining.

The hallway led to a flight of metal stairs that dropped through the main floor and into the tunnels. Luc had to duck under support beams, the weight of the bag throwing him off balance. There were small piles of rubble that spilled into the passageways from where connecting tunnels had been collapsed.

It was dark and Luc stumbled, trying to keep pace with Dolly, using her dim outline as a guide. "How can you see down here?"

"The implant provides outlines of everything. They really are amazing. I'd suggest it if you weren't leaving." Dolly glanced back. Luc noticed a glint in the one eye. "That reminds me. How are you planning on getting out of the city? With the slums empty and Dmitri on the hunt, I doubt they're letting people just stroll through the checkpoints."

Luc grunted. "I'm working on it. There aren't many choices."

"Holy crap." Dolly stopped and Luc nearly bumped into her. "You're going to try to get out at the mine exit." She walked away, leaving Luc to catch up.

"It's the only thing I can come up with. Tri said the broadcast is somewhere beyond the mines, anyway. I was planning on finding a place to lay low and look at the files you gave me then come up with something from there."

"Tri's right, but I've got some bad news."

"Yeah?" Luc huffed, struggling to keep pace.

"The station is far. It would take you weeks to get there by foot and you know what the wastes are like. No vegetation, no cover. If the Consortium was looking for you out there, it won't take them long."

Luc thought he could see Dolly gesturing with her hands, but he couldn't make out the motions. "I'll think of something."

Dolly clicked her tongue. "I really shouldn't help you. I'm still mad, and this raid is going to be a pain in my ass. Do you know how expensive bribes can get?"

"I can't say that I do, but I'd gladly take whatever help you are willing to offer."

"God, you're infuriating, Luc. I want to hate you so much, but I know you're just a buffoon trying your best. It's kind of like watching a bug struggle to right itself when it somehow managed to get stuck on its back. If it were scurrying, you'd just squish it." Dolly clapped her hands. "But when it's helpless…you know what I mean?"

"I'm not really in a position to argue, but I understand the sentiment." Luc stepped on a chunk of rock and stumbled.

"Hey. Who's taking your guitar?"

"Tri. She's getting my desktop computer too."

Dolly clicked her tongue again. "Too bad. I could have traded for that guitar."

"You don't give a shit about that guitar."

Shaking her head, Dolly turned down a side corridor. "No, but I know how much it means to you. I was going to smash it. I'm mostly interested in payback at this point. Maybe if I can hurt you, I'll get over it, ya know."

Luc snorted. "You could always kick me in the nuts."

Turning, Dolly pointed at him. "Hey! I could do that!"

"I was joking."

"It might do the trick, though." Dolly tipped her head to the side.

Shifting the bag, Luc hunched his back against a

cramp. "You can't be serious. We're in a tunnel running from Consortium officers."

Dolly waved a hand at him. "They're not going to find us down here." She shrugged. "Maybe when we resurface. It depends on if Dmitri thinks you're here or not. I'm guessing he's going to go all out searching for you. He never liked you spending time with his sister. Anyway." Smiling, Dolly rubbed her hands together. "We doing this or what?"

"The kick?"

"Yeah."

Luc put the bag down. "Do you really think this will help you forgive me?"

"I'm willing to try."

Luc sighed and Dolly hopped into a swing, bringing her foot into his crotch.

"Too late!"

Collapsing to his hands and knees, Luc gagged. "Come on," he said between coughs. "You didn't even let me get ready."

Dolly patted his back. "But that would defeat the whole point, RadDude."

Luc pushed himself up. His eyes were watering and he could feel a throbbing pain as far back as his tailbone. Reaching out to the wall, he steadied his wobbling legs. He let out a groan. "Is that it? Are we square now?"

"I'm not going to lie. That felt pretty good."

"Dolly." Luc heaved and spat, feeling the coffee churn in his empty stomach.

"I'm definitely getting there." With a smile, Dolly spun on one foot. "We're almost out of here. Let's go, I'll lead you past the guards and then I have a present for you." She looked back at him. "Huh. Maybe I am over it."

Broadcast Wasteland

Nineteen
On the City

The tunnels led up into the colony ship in the centre of the district. They crawled under deck panels, Luc pushing his backpack in front and dragging Dolly's overloaded bag behind him. The interior was musty and warm. Dampness clung to everything like the early morning mist.

Luc waited by a hatch while Dolly crept out into a hallway and made sure they were alone.

"All clear," she called. Her voice reverberated through the metal and was punctuated with her heavy footfalls as she hurried back. Putting out a hand, she helped Luc up and took his bag from him.

"Any way we can see out of this thing?" Luc brushed off his pants and picked dust bunnies from his jacket.

"I have sensors tied into my implant and can monitor my cameras set up, basically across the city."

Luc nodded. "Impressive."

Dolly slung his bag over one shoulder and practically bounced down the corridor. "It's a pretty rudimentary setup. Not much more than the kind of thing we built back in our clubhouse as teenagers—just more money, more time, and upgraded tech."

Pressing his lips together, Luc took a sharp breath through his nose. "Still very neat."

Dolly smiled. "I'm glad things aren't, you know, shitty, between us. It makes me kind of disappointed that we cleared the air just before you make a move like this."

"You think it's a bad idea." Luc held the handles of her bag in both hands. It swung like a pendulum as he walked.

"It's pretty desperate. I guess I can see your reasoning. Your place was always at the fringe. Ever since the Consortium took over."

"I suppose you're right." Luc ducked under a bulkhead and peeked through an open door. The curve of the ship made the ceiling drop sharply towards the end of the room. Some open crates were tipped on their side, a plastic tarp pulled back into a heap beside them. "This place is kind of sad."

Dolly shrugged. "Once it was abandoned, people got in and scavenged what they could. Squatters held up in here for a while, but Shadow and I put them to work. I debated putting something in here, a club or a coffee shop." Stopping, Dolly curled a lip and surveyed another room.

Luc looked over her shoulder. Wires hung from a panel in the ceiling and something scuttled for cover. "Why didn't you?"

"Not smart to spend money on something you can't own." Tapping him on the chest, Dolly moved on.

"So you own the warehouse?"

"Through circuitous means. Shadow and I do."

"That's really cool." The hall reached a corner and the ceiling plummeted. Luc crouched, sticking to where the ceiling was highest. "Did Shadow change, or…"

"Or. I just got good at working with him. I can anticipate his reactions to things and his motivation has always been unwavering."

"Money."

Chuckling, Dolly slowed, looking up and to the side. "Sure, but as a means to be in charge. I wouldn't say power specifically, but control, I guess." She pointed down an adjoining hallway. "This way. Security is starting to move away. They have their hands full with my customers."

"Sorry about that." Luc cringed.

"Yeah, yeah." Dolly took a deep breath. "So, do you think you'll find what you're looking for out there?"

Luc ducked under another bulkhead. "I had what I wanted. A little anonymity, intercepting the broadcast and sharing it with people, enough cash to keep my head down and dream of bigger things. I was happy." He sighed. "It felt like freedom."

"Then why run?"

"Dmitri is definitely going to send me to the mines. It's only a matter of time."

"That's the only reason?" Dolly's voice pitched up and she drew out the words.

"Anna wanted to go." Luc dropped the bag. "Sorry. I need a sec. This is heavy."

Dolly sat on the floor, leaning against the curved wall. "We got a sec." She picked at a nail. "Why do you think she wants to go?"

Luc squatted. "She doesn't see Dmitri's position for what it is."

"Yeah?"

"Sure." Luc stretched his shoulder. "It means being close to the Consortium, but it also means opportunity. With a little time and training, she could get a job that could take her off this colony. Maybe even get her to Earth."

"Then, why is she so against it?"

"She doesn't want to leave me behind." Luc looked away.

Dolly picked up a bolt and tossed it at him. "You know she likes you, right? Like, she always has?"

Letting the bolt land next to him, Luc nodded. "Well?"

"I, uh. I don't know how I feel."

"Aww, you suck." She cupped her hands around her mouth. "Boo."

"I don't want to hold her back. I don't want to… " He licked his lips. "I want everything. I want her, I want things to be the way they are. I—"

"You're afraid of commitment. I can't believe it. How lame." Dolly held out her hand. "Break time's over. We should get moving."

"Ugh. Yup." Luc reached out and they pulled each other up. "Is there a way to get by these guards?"

"Yeah, but there's a bigger problem."

Grabbing the bag, Luc heaved it over a shoulder, the handle in both hands. "What's that?"

"They've started raiding everywhere." Tapping her temple, Dolly watched her projection. "Oh, shit."

"What?" Luc tried to see what she was looking at, but remembered the projection was inside her eye.

"It's end of days out there. I'm getting SOS and warnings on all the boards. I don't know where you were planning on meeting with Anna, but the diner's a bust and they probably got your place too."

"Damn it." Luc clenched his jaw. "We have a

backup, but it's vague. Near the mining exit."

"Well, if she's there, and you can find her, that works in your favour. I think I can help you get some transportation." Dolly pointed at him. "Maybe."

Twenty
Wrong Side of Town

Luc ran down the back alleys of the downtown core, stopping at each corner to make sure there were no Consortium officers waiting to catch him. The night was cold and the wet air stung with tiny shards of ice that collected on his eyelashes. Dolly had transferred another file to his computer before she took off to find Shadow and plan how to survive Dmitri's raids.

They had parted with a hug and Luc told her to take what she wanted from his apartment, if the place hadn't been ransacked by security first.

Stopping at the crest of a pedestrian overpass, Luc crouched in the shadows of a support pillar. He had seen shuttles combing the colony, their spotlights shakily scanning the ground below them. There wasn't a pattern that he could tell, but he guessed most, if not all of them, were on patrol. A security cruiser sped down the road below him, lights flashing but with the sirens off.

Luc caught his breath and mentally went over the path between where he was and the exit to the mines. He took as straight a route as possible from the warehouse district, cutting through the heart of the city, but the tall buildings were to his back and apartments, businesses, and side streets were between himself and his goal. He thought of Anna, hoping she had found their supplies and was hiding somewhere near the checkpoint, but he wasn't sure how he'd find her.

Another shuttle flew overhead a few blocks to his right, skimming the buildings, its light swinging wildly in elliptical arcs.

Blowing into his hands, Luc waited for the ship to fly away and ran across the bridge.

The neighbourhood on the other side was rundown. The juxtaposition next to downtown was striking. Piles of crumbling façade littered the sidewalks below decomposing buildings. Broken strands of caution tape danced in the wind, tied to tipped barrels meant to block off certain alleys or the worst of the damaged buildings.

The few people that Luc saw were wearing old coats and shambled aimlessly. They were all hunched, beaten down by the corporation and its stranglehold on the colony. The neighbourhood closest to the mine was never a prime location. The noise and smell from the nearby mining operations brought down the value while the proximity meant that the workers, the poorest settlers, made it their home.

The takeover by the Consortium reinforced the stigma. When the mine started to dry up and the pay along with it, things compounded. It was the bad part of town in a city filled with poverty and crime.

Luc stuffed his hands in his pockets and kept his hood up. He walked quickly, balancing speed and conspicuousness. The few other people around him kept their distance, as if they could feel that he was the target of the guards who were searching the city in earnest.

Blinking away the wet ice, Luc cut down a side street, but kept close to the main road that led to the checkpoint. He debated trying to message Anna but didn't think he could find a secure channel. Instead, he hoped she was keeping an eye out for him and they would find each other by chance.

He figured the best place to start was as close to the checkpoint as he could get. Rushing down the narrow, cracked street, he watched for the spotlights overhead and the flashing lights on security cars—ready to bolt or hide. The houses were rundown and half of them had signs on the doors marking them as condemned. There was little more than broken and flattened fences in the neighbourhoods other than the odd abandoned vehicle. On a colony, material was too valuable to leave much besides rusted shells.

Luc saw a ship fly by a few blocks away and decided to change direction. He turned towards the main road, but stopped at the sight of flashing red on the roof of a cruiser. He hunched his shoulders and approached the nearest house, hoping it looked like he lived there. The vehicle turned away from him and drove off.

Realizing he had been holding his breath, he huffed and swallowed the built-up saliva. Once back on the street, he realized that he was a few blocks from the checkpoint. Small densely packed houses were butting up against apartments and stores that lined the major roads. Luc cut through a yard and onto the lot of an old gas station with a single repair bay facing the outer street that ran the circumference of the colony. The buildings across the road hugged the city wall giving way to the checkpoint nearby.

Most of the windows in the gas station were broken, and the few sets of shelves inside were tipped onto their side. He noticed an old cash terminal smashed on the floor and refrigerator missing its glass front.

Luc crouched at the back of the building and made sure there was no line of sight to him from the roads. Pulling up his sleeve, he checked his watch. It was close to midnight. He had no idea what the mining schedule was anymore. Even with the yields diminishing, people's desperation and the Consortium's decision to use prisoners to mine meant there were more shifts than before.

He heard a whistle and looked up. Scanning the vacant house, he shifted onto the balls of his feet and prepared to run.

"Up here."

Luc craned his neck and spotted a figure hanging over the edge of the gas station roof.

"It's me. Get up here."

"Anna?" Luc whispered. He shuffled away from the wall to get a better angle.

"Yeah. Hurry." She waved and pointed to a ladder attached to the side of the building.

Luc climbed up and saw Anna crouched next to an old air conditioner that had been stripped. The housing was mostly empty and some worthless parts were strewn about the roof.

"Come on. The ships have been flying over like crazy." She crawled into the unit and sat cross-legged.

Skulking over to her, Luc ducked, squeezing himself inside. He had to bend forward to fit and use his arms to get his legs to cross. "I'm so happy you're okay. What are the odds we'd run into each other?"

Anna shifted to give him more room. She picked up her bag and put it in her lap. "I know. I went back to your apartment. I guess Tri had been there because the radio, computer, and guitar were gone. She sent me a warning, so I went to the diner. I figured I could keep a better lookout from there and I could slip out the back if any guards came looking for me."

"I guess they did?"

Reaching out, Anna helped pull Luc into a sitting position. "You won't believe it, but Skeeter and his gang caused a distraction. Sasha ran in and told me to get out the back."

"Wow. They were actually good for something."

Anna shrugged. "I guess the enemy of my enemy."

Luc tried to nod, but his head was crammed against the ceiling.

"Anyway. I slipped out the back and worked my way here. I figured you'd take the shortest route and hope to be able to hide." Anna waved her hands as she detailed her thought process. "Assuming we would need a visual of the checkpoint, I started by getting as close as I could, then I worked back, looking for a place where we could hide. And here we are."

Clearing his throat, Luc popped his head out of the empty air conditioner. "That's way more thought out than my plan." A shuttle stopped over a street in the next neighbourhood and another went to join it. "It looks like your brother pulled the trigger. Hopefully security will be busy with the gangs and hackers they can find and we can slip out the back door."

"About that. What's next?"

Luc ducked back inside. The tiny pellets of ice pinged off of the cold metal. "Dolly came to the rescue. She had access to the worker passports. I just have to write up some ID signatures for the scans and with some luck we should be able to slip in on the next shift."

"You can do that?"

Digging out his computer, Luc banged his elbow into the wall. It bonged and resonated. "I think so. This thing should be more than powerful enough to send out two signatures. I still have to dig through the files Dolly gave me. Between my programs and hers, we should be able to pull it off."

"What can I do?" Anna took her own pocket computer out of her bag. It was covered in stickers, the exposed plastic a faded black.

"You can go over the maps from Tri and the location data from Dolly. Hopefully with their info we can find the broadcast source." Luc fished out a cable and plugged one end into his computer, handing the other end to Anna.

She smiled. "I can definitely do that."

"Great." The ice on his lashes was melting and Luc wiped it away. "Whoever finishes first can figure out the override program Dolly gave me so we can try to steal a mining vehicle to cross the wasteland."

Anna plugged in the cable and looked up at him, her eyebrows furrowed. "I guess she's over the whole software thing."

"Yeah. All it took was a little physical violence." Luc smirked and transferred the files to Anna.

Twenty-One
A Way Out

Luc stretched his back the best he could while in the cramped air conditioner housing. He and Anna had straightened their legs out, hers next to him on the inside of the unit, his, still bent, closer to the opening. The shuttles continued to fly overhead and the sound of sirens rose and fell as cruisers drove up and down the streets. His pocket computer in one hand, he held his finger over the enter key, ready to launch the ID program he'd written.

"If this works, I can tie the signals to the digital passports in the database and we can join the next shift going through the checkpoint."

Anna took a deep breath. "About that."

"Yeah." Luc looked up, but kept his finger in place.

"I was thinking, we can't just wander through the door dressed like this. Even in the middle of the other workers, we'll stand out like," she gestured to both of them, "like us."

"That's a good point, but it doesn't matter if the signal doesn't work. Can we put a pin in it and add it to the pile of things we still have to figure out?"

Nodding, Anna brought up her computer. "Sure. I'm ready to go."

Luc clenched his teeth. "Okay." He pressed the key and a little animation of two circles radiated outwards.

"I've got one." Anna bit her lip. "And I've got two."

Sighing, Luc turned off the transmission and looked for an open network uplink. "Great. I'll see if I can back my way into the network unnoticed and get this locked in. How are you coming on the maps?"

Anna scratched her head. "I think I've got it. Dolly had the actual coordinates, but I've had to find them on Tri's maps. The numbers don't seem to correspond, but I've been able to narrow it down to a pretty small area." She glanced up at him. "About twice the size of the city. That's good if the signal is coming from one of the terraforming plants, bad if it's a little shack or a small ship. We should be able to search in a grid if we can get to the area, though."

"That's great." He gave her ankle a squeeze. "We're making progress."

Anna swallowed. "I hope so. We've been in the same place for nearly an hour and they're still out there looking for us."

Luc nodded. "Yeah. But they have a whole city to search. We still have to figure out how to hack the vehicles, but if it's anything like hacking a car, we can make it work."

"We have to blend in, too."

"That or slip into a truck and hide in the back. I doubt they'll stop and search them."

"That could work." Anna bumped him with her knee. "We're close. I'm starting to get nervous."

"Me too."

The searchlight from a shuttle slowly approached, moving over the gas station. Luc tightened his grip on Anna's ankle and squinted, as if the beam would scorch him as it passed overhead. The ship didn't slow down, and the light faded away.

Anna let out a held breath. "When's the next shift? We have to go as soon as we can."

"Yeah." Luc finished connecting to the wireless network for a nearby apartment building and checked the Consortium website for the mining shift times. The next one was due at two in the morning. "Shit. Fifteen minutes."

"No time to find a uniform. We'll have to try your truck idea."

"Okay. Get as good a look at the vehicle hacking

program as you can. I have to get our IDs in the system." Luc focused on his screen.

"Uh huh."

Luc heard the clicks from Anna typing but as he focused on gaining access to the Consortium mining database, the sound blended in with the ice that pelted the metal air conditioner shell. Using his old programs and some of the codes he got from Tri and Dolly, he managed to get in through an employee email portal, then into the records for the cleaning crews at the downtown offices, and eventually to the Mining equipment manifests. Even the manifest was under a basic encryption. Luc tried to imagine what kind of computer could crack the main database—and which of the corporations could build such a thing.

Tucking his thumbs into his hand, he squeezed, cracking the knuckle. The cold caused his nose to run and the small of his back was numb from being pressed against the bottom of the metal housing.

He found the employee records Dolly had made, adjusted some of the information, and tied them into the ID signature produced by his pocket computer. The signal was meant to mimic the badges worn by the miners and implanted under the skin for prisoners—though the prisoners rarely came back into the city after being sentenced.

"I've gone over the vehicle access code."

Luc looked up and saw Anna cover one of her ears with her palm. The other was bright red.

"I think I can make it work, but I won't know until we try. It's a lot more complex than the simple consumer vehicle hotwire app." She sniffed. "It can cycle through known signals to replicate the key fob, though. It'll either work or not."

Reaching out, Luc took her hand. "Thank you. I know this is shitty."

Anna smiled. "It's just a little cold. We should go. How did you do?"

Nodding, Luc pulled his hand back. "I got it. I think. It's the same thing, right? It's going to work, or it won't. Nothing we can do now but try."

"Okay." Anna put her computer in the pocket of her canvas jacket and closed her backpack.

Luc followed her lead. He set the ID program to transmit and put his computer away. Peeking his head out of the cramped hiding place, he did a scan for the spotlights from shuttles and the spinning flash from a cruiser beacon. "All clear."

Icy snow had collected in a thin sheet on the roof. It was wet, soaking into his pants as he pulled himself out. He groaned as he moved from a kneeling position to a crouch.

"Sore?"

"Yeah." He chuckled. "Tight space."

"That reminds me." Reaching into her bag, Anna

pulled out a pair of synthetic leather gloves the same brown as his jacket.

"Those must have cost you a fortune. Easily more than you get from a week working with me." Luc left them hanging in the air in front of him as she held them out.

"You asked for gloves."

"I didn't mean those."

Anna pushed them into his chest and let go. "That sounds like a you problem."

Luc caught them before they fell. "Thank you, but it's too much."

Anna was half-way to the ladder. "You spent most of your savings on that computer and gave your stuff away."

Following, Luc looked over his shoulder and saw a ship between them and the tall buildings at the centre of the city. Beyond it were others, flying off over the neighbourhoods. "The computer was for me."

"It was for us, and we're leaving because of me too." Anna climbed over the edge of the building and descended out of sight. "I'm not going to keep talking about it. We're about to try to sneak past the checkpoint pretending to be miners." She peeked back over the edge. "And I don't look like a miner."

"Fine." Luc stuffed the gloves in his bag and climbed after her, stepping off the ladder onto crunching snow. His leg was tight from hiding in the air conditioner housing and his knee hurt. Snow had collected on the sparse bushes and over the toppled fence. It clung to the roofs of the houses but had melted on the roads.

Through the broken windows on the gas station, he saw a few miners heading towards the checkpoint. Behind them, a truck rolled up to the end of the street, waiting for a break in the traffic.

"That's our cue," Anna said, tapping him on the arm. She confidently walked around the side of the building to the road.

Broadcast Wasteland

Twenty-Two
Declarations and Threats

Several dozen people, most of them in dirty coveralls, shambled towards the small street that led past the checkpoint and off to the mine. A few of the hunched individuals mumbled a conversation, but the majority moved towards their inevitability in silence.

Luc pulled his hood up and made sure to keep pace with the largest group of miners. They spilled over the sidewalk and onto the road taking more than a single lane even with the large trucks driving past. The backs of the trucks were filled with tools and supplies, but mostly workers. Labour was cheap in the colony, but materials were limited.

Staying a step behind Anna, letting a few people fill the space in between, Luc made sure to keep his companion within the bubble of the ID transmitted by his computer.

She moved farther away from the guards who were lazily watching the procession next to a portable terminal automatically checking the miners. The big door was open, and the people were passing through it with the vehicles rather than going through the narrow halls inside the city wall to be processed one at a time.

Watching the soldiers out of the corner of his eye, Luc held his breath. The woman, who was balancing the laptop-like scanner on one of the railings, had a vacant gaze, her head tilted to the side. Luc could almost see the reflection of the screen in her glassy eyes. The rotund man next to her had one hand on the rifle slung over his shoulder and gestured with the other one. Whatever story he was telling his partner was likely causing her to zone out.

"Thank you, fat guard," Luc mumbled through his teeth.

The miner in front of him turned. "What did you call me?"

Luc glanced up but kept his face low. "Nothing. I was talking to myself."

"I don't recognize you. It your first night or something?" The man had soot in the wrinkles around his eyes, as if he were no longer able to fully scrub it away. He was missing at least one tooth and he wheezed as he spoke. "We got too many as it is. You should just head back and get some job with the corporation or something." He spat on the ground, the black saliva staining the snow gathered at the edge of the sidewalk.

"Leave the boy alone," another miner said out of the side of her mouth. "He's just looking for work like the rest of us."

"No! I don't gotta put up with more of these scrubs horning in on things. Them criminals are already too much. I'm going to find a new vein, not one of these snakes."

"Calm down, Heinrich," a third miner said.

Heinrich pointed at Anna through the bodies. "Look, there's another one. There's no room for you! Go back to mommy and daddy."

The woman who had spoken up first poked Heinrich in the belly. "What if she ain't got no mother, you insensitive prick?" She turned to Anna with a pout. "It's okay, sweetie. We know how hard it is out here."

"What's going on over there?" The fat guard had both hands on his shouldered weapon and was scanning the crowd.

Luc ducked, pushed through to Anna, pulled her down, and headed for an oncoming truck.

"We got scrubs horning in on our jobs," Heinrich yelled to the guard. "How come you let more and more snakes into the mine when there isn't enough for us as it is? You're the ones starving us. I haven't had a decent meal in weeks."

"Cut it out or we'll call in security," the woman at the scanner said.

Her partner jeered. "We ought to, just to shut up these ungrateful leeches."

"I don't need that kind of paperwork. They're already letting that prick hacker run-amok. This whole colony will be going to the dogs soon enough. May as well enjoy the ride while we can."

The commotion caused by Heinrich was kept to the three or four miners around him. The rest of the browbeaten colonists kept their heads low. They hardly noticed Luc and Anna pushing through them.

The truck was moving slightly faster than the people, its wheels as high as Luc's shoulder. He slipped under the vehicle, shuffling forward on his bent legs and a stabilizing hand. Anna, next to him, was short enough to hunch over and walk beneath the massive undercarriage.

They passed the gate and the road widened drastically. The truck picked up speed as it angled away from the pedestrians. It left them behind, but they were far enough away from the checkpoint to mix back in with the miners unnoticed.

The road to the mine curved away from the city and into foothills that flanked it like a canyon. It descended as they got closer to the mine itself, dug down to ease the elevation change over a long distance. The walls rose up on both sides, the rock becoming jagged slabs with deep grooves where the machines sliced into it. The lights from the city faded, leaving the headlamps and flashlights some of the miners carried, and the occasional passing vehicle, as the main sources of light. The pale moon with its fractured satellites was obscured by the canyon walls and the clouds still dusted the miners with ice pellets.

Luc and Anna moved along with the group, staying close to the centre. He wanted to keep away from Heinrich but he couldn't make out the man in the darkness.

In the distance, at the bottom of the road, the walls opened up. A huge pit that could fit several colonies in it spiralled into the ground. Spotlights around the edge shone into it, a mix of dust and ice swirling in front of them. A huge boom shook the walls and ground. Luc grabbed Anna's hand.

She gave it a squeeze. "I didn't expect a big hole in the ground like this."

Luc nodded.

The woman who had stood up to Heinrich came into view. She had been walking next to them and they hadn't noticed. "It can be intimidating, but if you keep your head on straight, you should be okay. This is just the first part of the mine. There's a lot more that are just tunnels in the ground all across the valley. The Consortium dug this out after the first vein dried up. They decided to dig out the whole thing and get as much valuable stuff as they could. It's dangerous, but not as bad as some of the deeper tunnels."

"Dangerous?" Luc asked.

"Any mining comes with risk." The woman held up her hand. Three fingers were missing. "Usually pit mining isn't as bad, at least not with cave-ins, but being so deep in the ground already, the blasting can cause avalanches." She nodded to the walls that rose up into darkness above them. "It's almost easier in the dark. They don't seem to lean in on you so much."

Anna smiled. "Thank you."

"Katrina." The woman put a hand to her chest. "You remind me of my little girl. I haven't seen her in many years."

Luc felt Anna stiffen next to him. He caressed her hand with his thumb. "You must miss her."

"Oh." Katrina turned away. "I do. Very much."

As they reached the end of the road, the narrow walls curved outward at different angles. A roughly circular plateau separated the road from the pit. It was big enough for the trucks that were jockeying to head back up the road and the three-story building that sat off to the side. More guards were standing in front of the building as the miners approached.

They wore full armour and helmets with blacked-out facemasks.

An administrator and her assistant were standing in the middle of a line of ten officers. The soldiers had their weapons drawn but pointed down at the road.

Luc noticed a few small, personal transportation pods parked at the side of the building. He nudged Anna and she nodded.

The administrator waved her hand and the guards fanned out, imposing themselves between the miners and the pit. The workers at the back of the line piled up and started to push. Their shift was starting soon, and Luc guessed none of them wanted a black mark on their company file.

Someone yelled for the people at the front of the pack to move forward and everyone jostled to get farther ahead.

The administrator waved her hand and her assistant picked up a portable speaker. He passed a microphone to her and lifted the speaker over his head.

Tapping on the mic, the woman gave a test blow and cleared her throat. "It has come to my attention that there is a special operation under effect. All known cyber criminals in the colony are being rounded up for interrogation and incarceration. There are still several reprobates who are yet to be found. The slackers who work the checkpoints are less than useless, but let it be known that the administrator of the mines of TRAPPIST Colony will not allow one of these criminals to hide in her mines under her watch."

She waved her hand again and the soldiers shifted position. The ones in the middle moved back, creating a funnel.

"Effective immediately. All incoming workers are to be individually scanned and searched upon entering the mining camp. Similarly, they will be checked back out again. Random searches will be carried out on site. You are expected to halt all operations and assist the soldiers with whatever they require of you. If you are found harbouring one of these, or any other criminal, known or otherwise, you will be treated as an accomplice and placed under arrest. However." The woman smiled, her crooked teeth highlighted by her dark lipstick. "If you turn in a wanted criminal, you will be rewarded."

Handing the microphone back to her assistant, she turned and headed for the building. The assistant fumbled with the speaker and microphone, nearly dropping both. After he managed to put them down, he waved over another guard who carried a terminal and hand scanner to the end of the funnel.

Anna patted Luc on the shoulder and pointed to Katrina. The old miner had a hand to her chest and looked as if she were going to faint. He reached out to steady her, but she put her arm between them.

"Are you okay?"

"I'll be fine. Just heartbroken."

Moving Luc aside, Anna put her arm around the woman. "Is that your daughter?"

"No. But she was her friend." Katrina set her gaze on the retreating director and the unsteadiness was replaced with rage. She shook with it. "That monster betrayed my sweet girl in order to get into the position she is now. She got there on the blood and toil of all of us!"

Katrina's yelling drew attention to them. Luc hunched down and peered through the taller miners. A few of the guards were looking, but most were focused on funnelling the group to the scanner. Some of the other miners were taking notice, though. One or two murmured their assent and directed more towards the commotion.

"We have to go." Luc pulled Anna away from Katrina.

"Where?"

Luc stood on his tiptoes and looked back up the road. "I don't know. Maybe try to get to the back at least. Buy some time. As soon as they see us, they'll know we don't belong here."

Anna grabbed him by the sleeves and pulled him lower. "And this poor woman?"

Sighing, Luc scrunched his face. "I understand.

I feel for her too, but we couldn't do anything to help her even if we weren't on the run."

Anna frowned. "Okay. Priorities."

Luc peeked over the crowd again. Katrina was wailing and pushed her way towards the building.

"You're a monster," she screamed. "You're a cold-hearted tyrant who steps on us for your own gain."

More of the crowd was responding to her shouts, nodding and bellowing in agreement. The guards looked uneasy, shifting their weight and looking at one another. The assistant seemed to notice and moved from his spot at the opening of the funnel.

"Calm down or you'll regret it." He stood well behind the soldiers like a child taunting a sibling from the safety of his mother's ankles. "I'm warning you!"

Luc grabbed Anna by the wrist and charged for the road, but the tide of people surged against him.

"Wait!" Anna had her computer out. She pulled her arm free and flipped the screen open.

"No time. This is getting ugly, fast." Luc did his best to root himself to the spot, forcing miners to flow around him.

"Hang on. I'm doing something."

Gritting his teeth, Luc felt his boots slip in the dirt and snow and dug in deeper. Through the milling bodies, he saw one of the guards bring up his rifle. "We're out of time."

Over the jeering of the crowd he heard the assistant yelling for them to stop and Katrina hurling insults. Some of the miners still seemed not to know why they had been stopped and were yelling to be allowed to get to work, but most of them were caught up in anger and frustration at how they had been treated, joining in on Katrina's outrage.

A set of bright lights washed over the crowd. Luc saw them as dappled through the still churning mass. Wedges of it caught his eyes through arms and legs, making him squint.

"Anna! Come on!" His foot slipped and he fell, tripping Anna who landed on top of him. Luc heard a shot and rolled on top of her. The crowd recoiled as one. Someone fell onto him and another stepped on his hand. Steadying his legs, he stood, forcing his way up, helping Anna stand with him. He heard more shots and flinched, waiting for a bullet to rip through the miners and hit him, but the mob surged forward again, taking him and Anna with them. He turned and saw that most of the soldiers were facing the opposite direction—at an incoming personal transport pod that raced towards them.

In the confusion, the miners attacked.

Broadcast Wasteland

Twenty-Three
Transportation

Pandemonium took over. The miners attacked the soldiers, the soldiers split their attention between the miners and the vehicle that had charged towards them, and Luc couldn't do anything other than hang on to Anna as they were carried into the fray.

He tried to plant his feet, to halt their tumble into danger. Grunting and squirming, he managed to slowly chip away at the surge until only a few haggard miners limped around them, following their comrades as quickly as they could.

Luc took a ragged breath and pulled his stepped-on hand close to his chest. His leg hurt and his knee popped when he put weight on it. "Shit."

Anna got under his arm, taking some of his weight. She turned them towards the commotion and tried to carry him back.

"Wait. Where are you going? We should leave.

Get to the end of the road and try to sneak around the canyon and out into the wasteland."

"No." Anna kept moving and Luc had to hop to keep up. "This way."

Scrunching his face, Luc hobbled along, unable to stop her. "They'll shoot us, those miners are as good as dead."

"I hope not." Anna grunted and adjusted her grip on him. "It would be my fault."

"No. You didn't do that. It was frustration boiling under the surface for years. It probably would have happened eventually." Luc clenched his teeth, putting some weight on his leg. "It doesn't matter now. We just have to get away while we can."

"That's what I'm doing."

"We're going the wrong way."

Reaching into her pocket, Anna took out her computer. She flicked it open with a thumb and managed to press a couple of buttons, the device teetering in her hand. The vehicle turned and drove around the miners towards them.

"Is that you?" Luc glanced down at her screen. There was a representation of the pod on the screen along with a set of controls and a smaller window that showed a view from inside the vehicle.

Anna nodded. She was biting her lip, struggling with carrying him and focusing on driving the pod towards them. "Get ready."

The car sped up as it approached. It was small with two front seats, a tiny jumper seat in the back that faced into the cabin, and a little truck bed on the back. The whole thing was just over two metres. The windshield was long and curved, starting above the front seats and arcing out and down to the low dashboard. The glass was marked where it was hit with bullets from when Anna drove it towards the guards. There was a hole in the passenger door and one in the bumper.

Luc glanced back at the growing chaos and saw one of the guards point towards them and try to get around the angry miners. Skidding to a stop next to them, the pod kicked up a mix of snow and dirt. Anna grabbed Luc around the waist, but he waved her off.

"Get to the driver's seat." He hobbled to the passenger side. Anna was sliding into the seat next to him as he pulled his injured leg into the cabin and closed the door.

There were no controls in front of the driver other than a few switches and a screen. It showed the same image as on Anna's computer but along with the forward camera view, it had a camera facing the rear as well.

Luc dropped his bag in the back along with Anna's and looked out the small rear window. The soldier who had spotted them took aim and fired.

The shot hit the tailgate and knocked it open. Before the guard could shoot again, one of the miners grabbed the rifle.

Using her computer, Anna drove them away from the plateau. Luc watched as the individual forms became a tangled mass with distance and darkness. The lights on the miner's helmets showed him snippets, but the road curved and the high walls cut off the scene.

"That was amazing." Luc held his knee.

"I'm just glad it worked." Anna split her focus between her computer and the view outside the windscreen. The small car was quick. The faint whine of the motors was drowned out by the crunching of gravel and slosh of snow as the little tires dug into the dirt.

"I'm sure they've already contacted the city soldiers by now. Our escape may still need some sorting out, but I'll bet the guards are on their way and will be on the lookout for the pod." Luc opened the small glove box. There was a flashlight, a pen, and some loose paper. He searched for other compartments, then turned in his seat and looked in the back.

"So, what do we do? Where am I driving?"

Under the bags, Luc found a tire iron, a jack, a battery charger, and a small solar kit. "Not much we can do but keep heading up this road. When we get to the end, just kill the lights and stick as close to the rock wall as possible. If we're lucky, we can slip past them before they mount some kind of operation."

"And if we meet them on the road?"

Luc settled back in the passenger seat. He scrunched his face. "We'll have to play it by ear?"

"Really inspired." Anna pointed at his seatbelt. "Buckle up."

The trip up the road was much faster in the vehicle. Glancing at his watch, Luc stifled a yawn. "How you doing? It's getting late."

"Huh?" Anna was fighting to keep them out of the ruts in the ground made by the bug trucks. "Yeah, I'm okay. What time is it?"

"After three."

A loose strand of hair dropped into her face and she blew it back. "Not too late—for us at least."

"I suppose not. I'm pretty tired, though." Luc shifted in the seat, tweaking his knee. He winced.

Grimacing, Anna risked a peek, though the cabin was dark. "Well, I didn't get stepped on. You okay?"

"Something's not right, but I'll live. Hopefully I just sprained it." He huffed. "Good thing you got us this pod. I wouldn't do well with walking right now."

The lights of the city started to glow over the top of the rock wall as they ascended. A shape flew towards them and a spotlight came on under it, pointed down at the road as it approached.

"Luc?" Anna pointed to it.

"Yeah. I see it."

"What should I do?" Grabbing her computer with both hands, it slipped and fell. The pod automatically applied the breaks and they skidded into one of the deep ruts left by the trucks. It slid farther into the groove, leaning sharply to the passenger side. "Shit!" Anna reached under her seat to get her computer.

"Kill everything," Luc said. He grabbed the dashboard and pulled himself closer to the screen in front of her and hit the ignition button. The pod powered down as the ship flew overhead. It kept its speed and was gone in a second, following the curving road to the plateau.

Luc sighed and let himself drop back to his side of the tilting vehicle. "Close call, but I think they're more concerned with the riot going on with the miners. There's got to be more of them on the way, though. Probably some cruisers or at least a truckload of soldiers."

Anna didn't reply. She was still leaning forward, her hands by her feet.

"Are you okay?"

Sniffing, she wiped away a tear. "Yeah… No."

"Hey." Luc rubbed her back. "We're okay. It's gone."

"I know. But." She heaved a shuddering breath. "I dropped the computer. We could have been caught."

"But we weren't. It was an accident that could have happened to anyone."

Anna nodded. "I know."

"You did a good job. We can't control what they do. We just have to try to stay one step ahead of them."

"I just." She leaned back. Her face was wet and a tiny snot bubble formed over her nostril. She wiped it with a sleeve. "I'm sorry. I'm gross."

Luc chuckled. "No." He took her face in his hands. "You're not gross. You're wonderful."

She leaned in and pressed her forehead to his. "I thought that was it. They caught us. Ya know?"

"Me too. But we still have a chance. We have to move, okay?"

Anna nodded, her head rocking against his. "Yeah." She leaned back and wiped her eyes with the palm of her hand. "What's the plan?"

Luc undid his seatbelt. "You get the engines going, I'll see if I can push us out of this rut."

"What about your leg?"

Smiling, Luc grabbed the door handle. "I think I'll be okay." The door swung open and he fell out.

Broadcast Wasteland

Twenty-Four
Out of the Rut

"I'm okay." Luc pulled himself up using the open door. He tried to brush the majority of the snow and muck off of his jacket. Most of it slid off in semi-frozen chunks. "Start it up."

He hopped to the back of the car, using the truck bed for support. One of the wheels was completely off the ground and the front passenger tire was half buried. Flipping up the tailgate, he gave the pod a test push, keeping his injured leg off the ground. It rocked, slightly, but his foot slipped in the snowy mud.

The lights flashed on and he heard the hum of the electric motors coming to life.

"On the count of three, give it a little power. I'll see if I can get it moving."

Anna had her door open. "Okay. Ready when you are."

Luc counted down and shoved. The wheels spun and the vehicle dug a little deeper into the muck. "Whoa! Stop!"

Cutting the power, Anna got out and surveyed their predicament. "Oh, crap. How are we going to get out of this?" She put her hands on her hips.

"You can control this thing from out here. Can you do it while pushing?" Luc leaned on the back of the pod.

Anna took out her computer. She held it and made a pushing motion. Shaking her head, she turned around and mimed leaning against the vehicle with her back. "I think so."

"Alright." Luc hopped back to the passenger door. "I'm going to get the tire iron and dig out the front wheel. Then we can both try pushing and you can give it some juice."

"We have to hurry. Maybe we should abandon it and just run."

Luc grunted as he leaned into the cabin and rummaged in the back seat. "I'm not running anywhere, and even if I wasn't injured I, uh, doubt we'd stand much of a chance crossing the wastes on foot."

"I guess." Anna kicked the pod and Luc heard some snow hit the ground. "They'd probably have an easy time catching up to us anyway."

"That's the spirit." Luc pulled out the tire iron

and crouched next to the buried tire. He used the bent end to dig away snow and mud from around it. "I think I'm making some progress. Want to give it a shot?"

"Sure."

He stood and dropped the bar into the front foot well then grabbed the door. "Ready when you are."

"One, two, three."

The tires spun and they both grunted with effort. The pod moved, the front tire pulling free from the mud. Luc lost his footing and slipped, rolling away.

The back tire on the passenger side hit the edge of the rut and slid to join the front wheel.

"Shit!" Anna cut the power.

Luc got to his good foot and lunged at the pod. "Don't stop! We're making progress."

The wheels spun again, kicking up the slurry of mud, snow, and ice. It pelted Luc as he threw his shoulder into the doorframe. "Left! Get it out of the rut!"

Anna turned the virtual wheel and the pod fought to climb out of the ditch.

Luc let it pull away from him and joined Anna at the back, limping to keep up. He grabbed under the back bumper and lifted as much as he could, grunting. The back wheel hopped out of the groove and the front end followed the momentum.

Driving it away from the rut, Anna stopped next to Luc and let him lean on her. "That did it. Good job."

Luc huffed. "Yeah. You too."

Hobbling to the pod, they both got in. Anna accelerated before they were buckled. She pulled the belt across herself as she steered with one hand.

Rubbing his hands on his pants, Luc leaned forward and peered out the windscreen. "Can you cut the lights?"

"Not unless we want to get stuck again." Anna focused on the scene in front of them—on what she could see illuminated in the headlights.

"Okay." Luc sat back and did up his belt. His hands were numb from digging in the muddy snow.

"Did you dig us out without wearing the gloves you asked me to buy for you?"

Shrugging, Luc rubbed his hands together. "I forgot. We were in a hurry."

Anna huffed.

The rock walls on either side of them were only a few feet higher than the top of the vehicle and the distance between them grew as the natural formation took over for the machine-dug path. The road smoothed out and there were fewer deep ruts.

"Okay. Now I can turn the lights off." Anna cut the headlights and increased their speed. The faint glow from the lights mounted along the outside of the city wall was enough to keep her from careening into rock.

"Good job. Keep to the left and follow the mountain as it curves away from the city." They hit a bump and Luc bounced out of the seat, the belt pulling him back.

"Sorry."

Luc wheezed. "It's okay." He bounced his uninjured leg, the pain in his other one temporarily ignored as they got closer to the checkpoint. If the guards were paying attention, they would see them for sure. If there were soldiers on the way to the mines, they should be heading towards them any moment.

Anna grunted. "I hate this feeling. My hands are shaking."

"I know." Luc touched her shoulder. "Just keep focusing on the ground in front of us."

She was looking more at the screen, watching the view from the camera mounted at the front. The rock wall next to them was replaced by rolling foothills—then they were out of the canyon.

Anna kept the speed up and they left the checkpoint behind, racing through the open space between the natural and human-made structures.

Turning around to look out the back window, Luc smiled. "I think we slipped past them."

Broadcast Wasteland

An alarm sounded and the big door started to rise.

Twenty-Five
Race

"Just couldn't keep your mouth shut, could you?" Anna leaned into a turn, sending the pod hurtling towards the mountain to their left. She straightened the pod out before they hit a rock outcropping. The tires and shocks thrummed under them, the vehicle bouncing along with the uneven ground.

Luc watched two cruisers turn off the road and head towards them—their sirens screaming and lights flashing red. "They're going to be on us soon."

"Can you do anything about that?" Anna said through gritted teeth.

"I don't think so."

"Then let me focus."

Following the mountain, they continued to get farther away from the city as the opposing curves diverged. They hit another bump and Luc was thrown into the door. A sharp pain shot through his knee, the injury coming back into focus.

Keeping an eye on the cruisers, Luc glanced over the receding city expecting to see a shuttle crest the buildings, but the sky remained empty. He hoped they were refuelling, giving the pod a chance to escape.

Anna abandoned the foothills and cut across the open wastelands, the ground levelling out. There were a few jagged mounds of rocks and several rough patches, but she avoided them.

One of the cruisers got behind the pod, the other one stayed behind and to the side of its partner. A code flashed across the screen and the pod lost speed.

"Luc?" Anna split glances between her computer and the scene out the windscreen.

"I see it." Leaning over Anna, Luc saw a remote shutdown warning blocking most of the controls. "Uh, I think I can stop this." Pressing a button in the corner of the screen, he brought up a virtual keyboard and started to work his way into the root files of the car.

Anna leaned back, using her pocket computer and its tiny screen to drive. "Switch spots!" She unbuckled both of them and slipped behind Luc.

Trying to keep a step ahead of the shutdown, Luc banged his bad knee while slipping into the driver's seat. "Ah! Damn it."

The pod jerked to the side as Anna settled next to him and pushed Luc's foot out from under her. "Sorry. I've got it."

Luc ignored her and found the location of the code that corresponded with the shutdown order. He attempted to delete the relevant data, but the warning still flashed and the pod continued to slow. "Shit."

Reaching under the dashboard, he pulled free the wiring harness.

"Do you know which one it is?" Anna asked.

"No idea. You?" Grimacing, Luc separated a bundle of wires and traced them from one side of the dash to the other. "I'm pretty sure it's the green one with white stripes, but I've never tried to steal this model before."

"Stole a lot of cars when I wasn't looking, did you?" Anna steered them around a rock and the cruiser behind them braked, backing off a bit.

"Once or twice." Luc swallowed holding the wire in his fingers. "I'm going to go for it."

Anna winced. "Not much choice."

Luc pulled the wire free, along with a purple one that he didn't notice was attached to it. "Shit." The pod surged forward and the screen went black. "Shit!"

Anna turned to her computer. "No. I've still got it here."

Sighing, Luc held his knee and looked over his shoulder. "One problem down, two still really close behind us."

"I have an idea." Anna bit her lip.

"Sounds good. I'm all for it."

Sucking in air through her teeth, she grimaced. "I'm not sure I can pull it off."

"Sweetie. I've got nothing, so I say give it a shot." Luc squeezed her leg.

"Alright, hang on." Leaning before the car turned, Anna sent them directly for a rock mound. It was one of the smaller ones, not much larger than their pod. The sharp tip of it was lower than the height of their windscreen.

"You see that, right?" Luc pushed himself into the seat and gripped the handle that protruded just above the door.

"Yup. But I hope they don't." Anna kept them charging towards the outcropping at full speed until Luc lost sight of where it broke through the ground. At the last moment, she swerved, throwing them to the right. She slipped out of the passenger's seat and into Luc's lap as the back end of the vehicle bounced off the rock. They fishtailed on the snowy ground as she fought to straighten them out.

There was a huge crunch behind them and Luc looked out the back window. One of the cruisers was stationary. He could make out the outcrop in between the headlights—bent inward by the impact.

Luc let out a whoop and wrapped an arm around Anna. "That was amazing."

The pod started to shake and Anna slipped back into her seat. "I think I broke something.

Leaning over the back seat, Luc took a closer look. The truck bed of their pod was dented inward and the tailgate was hanging open. "It doesn't look too bad."

The second cruiser slammed into them. The tailgate came loose on one side and bounced along with the shaking.

"What was that?" Anna had one hand on her computer bracing herself against the dashboard with the other.

"The soldier is pissed that we caused his buddy to wreck." Luc reached down by Anna's feet and grabbed the tire iron.

"What are you going to do?"

"I don't think I should tell you."

"Why not?"

He put a hand on the door handle. "Because you'll get mad at me."

Anna reached for him. "Then don't do it!"

Opening the door, Luc scrunched his face. "I'm sorry." He grabbed the roof and pulled himself out of the cabin.

"Luc! If you don't die, I'm going to kill you!"

The cold wind hit his face and stung his eyes. He couldn't tell if it was snowing or if the cars were kicking up what was on the ground. Pulling himself into the truck bed, he saw the Consortium vehicle charge at them again.

He threw himself onto the floor and grabbed a loop made for cargo straps as the pod jumped on impact. The tailgate slammed back against the bed and the loose end swung out, hanging over the ground.

The cruiser backed off, letting them get some space, likely planning to ram them again. The back of the pod shook where the bed was dented from the impact with the rock. Luc felt the thrumming through his arm as he gripped the side and shuffled to the back. He swung the iron down on the bracket keeping the tailgate attached, but it ricocheted back at him.

"Shit." His hands were already going numb and he remembered his brand-new gloves were still in his backpack. Taking a breath, he gripped the tire iron tighter and slammed it down again. The hinge opened wider, but it held on.

They hit a rut and the whole pod bounced. Luc was airborne for a moment and the vehicle almost drove out from under him. He reached for something to grab onto, dropping the tire iron. His legs dangled out the back as he clung to a loop.

Hearing the whine of the cruiser over the wind and crunching snow, he pulled and rolled into the truck bed just before the front end of the Consortium vehicle bashed into them for a third time. It backed off again, but Luc lost his grip. He put his injured leg out and stopped himself against the loose hinge.

He screamed in pain, pushing his other foot into the sidewall. "I can't keep this up." Gritting his teeth, he rolled onto his knee and took hold of the tailgate. With a grunt, he bent it straight up, snapping the weakened hinge. The sudden weight almost caused him to fall out, but he got his damaged leg underneath him. He threw the tailgate at the cruiser as it charged again. It hit the windscreen and bounced off, leaving a gouge in the glass and sending spiderweb cracks across the surface.

The car made impact, wedging its nose under the pod. Luc was half in the bed and half on the hood of the cruiser. He flipped onto his stomach to crawl back towards the cabin and his hand touched the tire iron.

"Okay." He breathed heavily and shivered in the freezing wind. Standing, Luc threw the tire iron as hard as he could towards the figure in the driver's seat. The flattened end stuck partway into the glass and the cruiser braked. The pod slipped off the hood and Luc fell onto his back.

The Consortium driver turned the wheel sharply and the cruiser hit a crevice. The front end dug into the ground and the back end flew into the air. It flipped and landed on its side with a huge crash, rolling forward with its own momentum.

Luc covered his mouth, watching pieces of the vehicle tear free and spin off in every direction. The car careened into an outcropping of rock and exploded in a fireball.

Crawling to the cabin, Luc opened the door and gingerly got back inside. When the door was closed, Anna turned to him.

"What was that?"

Luc grimaced. "I think I got him."

Twenty-Six
Rest a While

They drove through the night. The wobbling back tire hung on but shook more and more as the kilometres piled up. The sun was still behind the horizon, but its light created a haze, promising its arrival. The snow had stopped and they even found large fields where the bare rock was clean of it. Other than the occasional protrusions through the planet's thick crust and the mountain range that persisted to the south, there was nothing to block their view.

Luc took one of his extra shirts and the handle of the jack and made a splint, keeping his knee straight. He had to prop it up on his bag and sit as far back in his seat as he could. He had his computer out and was looking for a match on the topographical satellite image to pinpoint their location and make sure they were going in the right direction.

Anna kept them moving forward. They sped

through the night, the headlights off. As soon as the dawn was bright enough to show them the surrounding landscape, she cut back on the throttle. Yawning, she flexed her hands in turn. "We're at about a quarter battery reserves."

Keeping his gaze on his screen, Luc pointed out directions as he searched for their location. "That chase probably zapped a lot of juice." He looked up and pressed his lips together. Reaching out his hand, he touched her arm. "You did so well."

"If it weren't for you."

Luc waved the compliment away. "That was luck. Good for us, bad for him."

"You had to do it, Luc."

"I'm not thinking about it." He rubbed his eyes and sighed. "I'm more worried about them chasing us down. Even with this head start, their cars are faster than this thing at full power." Looking out the window behind them, he winced as his knee twitched. "And they'll find us eventually if they send those shuttles after us."

"I'm surprised they haven't already." Anna manoeuvred them around a boulder.

"Things must be more chaotic back in the city than we thought." He turned to face her. "Maybe they don't know where we are yet?"

"I've been trying to break up our tracks, heading for the areas without any snow." Anna nodded to the barren ground around them.

Luc pushed himself up in his seat to get a better look. "That's good thinking." He tapped his computer. "I'm still not sure where we are."

"We are heading west though, right?"

Nodding, Luc stretched. "The best I can tell. No idea if we're on track to find the source of the broadcast, though." Looking past her at the foothills, Luc noticed that they were levelling out. "We may be close to the end of this mountain range."

"Oh. That looks promising." Anna turned them towards the low hills. They were exposed rock, seemingly strung together like a giant cobblestone road. "That should hide our tracks nicely."

"We won't be able to keep up this speed. Especially with that wheel at the back."

Anna shrugged. "It may buy us more time if they're tracking us down."

Biting his lip, Luc looked behind them again. "Yeah. I suppose."

"You just worry about pointing us in the right direction. Let me handle the driving." Anna winked at him. "I've been doing alright so far."

Luc chuckled. "Yeah."

The foothills eventually vanished and the rock that pushed through the surface got bigger—some of them as tall as a two-story building. Anna had to take time to drive around them, avoiding dead ends and deep crevices.

Luc had gone through all the topographical satellite maps and was deep into the photographs of the surface, tracing their path from the city, across the wasteland.

"I think I found our location." He looked out at the towering spires and back to his screen. "I'm running low on battery."

"Me too." Anna tapped her computer against her palm. "And so is the pod."

The sun was above them, its light weaving through the space between the big, piercing rock mounds. Luc shifted in his seat, gritting his teeth as a pain shot through his knee. "We should probably stop. Find a place to set up that solar panel."

Anna nodded. Luc saw dark circles under her eyes. She blinked slowly.

He furrowed his eyebrows. "We should try to get some sleep too." Turning his attention to the scene around them, he tried to spot a place with some cover. "Maybe hide?"

"I think I see somewhere." Anna drove them to a place where one of the rock towers had apparently fallen over and was leaning against its neighbour. There was a hollow under them that looked like it was big enough for the pod to fit and the angle of the sun illuminated the space in front of it.

"That's perfect. Should provide cover from the air and this field is a maze."

The fit was tight, and Luc had to get out before Anna drove the pod into the cave. She brought out the solar panel and his gloves.

"You forgot these, again."

Luc half-smiled as he took them from her. "Thanks. It's cold. Like even more cold than around the city."

Nodding, Anna folded her arms. "Maybe we've slowly been going up hill?"

Luc shrugged and pulled on the gloves. His hands were instantly warm. "Oh. These are nice."

Anna fought a smile. "You're welcome."

"Thank you." He let his shoulders drop. "I'll set up the panel, can you run the cables?"

Nodding, Anna grabbed the charging cable and dragged it to the port on the vehicle.

His leg held straight, Luc carried the panel out into the sun. It was as tall as he was, but light, made of a stiff frame, the panels themselves, and a small box with the electronics. Shading his face, he watched the sun for a moment, predicting its path and the shadows that it would cast as it moved across the sky. He chose a spot where he thought the panels would get the most consistent energy and hobbled back to the pod.

Anna was crouched, inspecting the damaged rear

wheel. "We're plugged in and charging. Looks like it's going to take some time, especially with our computers drawing power, too."

Luc stopped next to her. "How's that looking?"

She grimaced. "Honestly, I'm not sure. Something is bent, but I have no idea what, or how to fix it."

Leaning over to get a closer look, Luc absent-mindedly rubbed her back. "Yeah. Got me there, too."

"Okay." Anna grabbed the side of the truck bed and pulled herself up. "Time to recharge." She poked him in the stomach. "That goes for us too."

"Ah." Luc stumbled back.

"Sorry." Wrapping her arm around him, she helped Luc get to the driver's door and into the pod. She followed in after him.

Luc took out his pocket computer and plugged it into a charging port in the centre console.

Anna did the same with hers. "I'm going to pass out in a minute." She yawned.

"Me too. I'm going to see if I can map out our route from here to where Dolly said the source is, though." Luc flipped open the screen on his computer.

"Don't stay up too long." Anna leaned her seat back as far as it would go and rolled onto her side, facing him. "We have to sleep while we can. We probably won't find another hiding place as good as this and we're not even that sure how much farther we have to go."

Luc scratched his head. "I won't. Just want to get a head start so we can go as soon as this thing is charged back up."

"Okay." Anna closed her eyes and rested her head in her hand.

Luc went back to the screen. He flexed his leg, wincing, then started to scroll through more satellite photos.

Broadcast Wasteland

Twenty-Seven
Long Horizon

Luc felt the ground tremble. He grunted as something bounced him up and down. With a snort, he opened his eyes. The world was moving around him. He blinked, swallowed, and realized that he was inside a Consortium pod being driven across the wastes. A scream welled inside him, but he cut it off as he spotted Anna in the driver's seat.

He remembered the previous day and blinked away the remnants of sleep. "We're driving."

"Uh huh." Anna had her pocket computer resting on the blank screen built into the dashboard.

The sun was streaming in behind them, steadily plunging towards the horizon. Luc leaned back and watched the long shadow of the vehicle mark the path ahead of them. "How long was I out?"

"Most of the day."

"And how long have you been driving?"

Anna glanced over at him and smiled. "A while. A good five hours or so."

Stretching, Luc felt a twinge in his knee. It was stiff, but not as painful as it had been the day before. "Why didn't you wake me?"

"You were sleeping. I thought it would be nice to let you get some rest."

"I wish you would have woke me up." Luc reached into his pocket to take out his computer, but it wasn't there. He patted the rest of his jacket but didn't feel it. Frantically, he checked again.

"I've got it here." Anna leaned back, showing his computer next to hers. "Had to use it for the map. You did a good job finding our location and marking out the path to the—well, the area where Dolly thinks the broadcast is coming from. The pictures are really helpful."

Luc swallowed and grimaced at the taste in his mouth. "Are you being sarcastic?"

Anna chuckled. "No." She put a hand on his leg. "Go ahead and freshen up. I picked up some toiletries and water. You should probably take a better look at that knee, too. There's a first aid kit in my bag."

"You really thought of everything." Shifting in his seat, Luc unbuckled and took off his jacket and hoodie.

"Just about." Anna pulled her hand away.

"How much juice do we have in the batteries?" Removing the splint and pulling down his pants, Luc winced at the sight of his knee. It was purple and black with bits of dried blood along the outside of the joint. He reached into the back of the cabin and grabbed both backpacks.

He disinfected his injury and wrapped it in bandages. Giving it a test bend, he clenched his jaw, but other than a disconcerting pop, he was able to move it without much pain.

Inside Anna's bag, he found a couple of toothbrushes, toothpaste, and a big package of wipes. "One of these for me?" Luc held up the toothbrush.

"Yeah. Go nuts, but use your own water. We only have so much."

"You're the best." Luc cleaned himself, using the wipes before pulling up his pants or putting on a new shirt. He brushed his teeth, spitting out the window. The wind was freezing. When he was fresh and bundled back up, he chugged most of his water.

"I'm sorry, I was so thirsty." Wiping his mouth with the back of his hand, he held the bottle out to Anna.

"Good thing I got us a few bottles each. I'm okay."

Luc buckled back up and surveyed the scenery. "How much farther do you think we have to go?"

Anna shrugged. "It's a few hundred kilometres

to the general area, but it's big. Could take us hours to find it once we get there. If it's even there."

"Want me to take a turn driving for a while?"

Shaking her head, Anna turned on the headlights. The mountain was far behind them, looming like a sleeping giant. It was like a physical barrier between them and the city, holding back the corporation as they fled. The ground around them was flat with no trace of the foothills that followed them out of the mountain range or the jutting rocks where they had hidden. Other than the few small mounds that looked like ancient craters, there was nothing to see.

"At least let me give the satellite photos another look. Maybe I can find some more clues." Luc held out his hand.

"Yeah, sure." Anna passed his computer to him. "Just make sure I'm staying on track. It's basically just west from here, but I've had a few detours around craters and hills and stuff."

"Okay." Luc leaned back in his seat and opened the files containing the photos. He skipped right to the large parameter that Dolly had marked. Starting with the assumption that the broadcast came from a facility, he skimmed the images from a high altitude. Eventually he was combing the ground from the height of the low flying shuttles with nothing to show for it.

"Ugh. There's nothing here." Letting his hands drop into his lap, Luc huffed and looked out the windscreen. "Dolly said the network was dropping in and out and that the satellites had been moved for some reason."

"Do you think that has something to do with Dmitri?"

Luc shook his head. "Probably not. That's pretty high-level stuff. Plus, it started before he made his move. I can't imagine why the Consortium would reposition their satellites." Leaning forward, he tried to look up out of the windscreen. "They already have the surface scanned and I'm sure they were already optimized to cover the colony."

"Could someone have hacked them?" Anna asked.

"I guess. It would take some serious skill and there's no way to hide it from the Consortium. They'd respond." Luc sat back. "I wish I knew what was going on up there. Maybe," Luc bit his lip, "maybe when we get there, to where the broadcast is coming from, we can try to contact one of the other corporations. Telbak, or even Amcoral."

"Think they'd come?"

Luc watched the view through the windscreen. "I don't know. Probably not."

The headlights cut through the darkness, showing a clear wedge of the landscape. It was still flat, empty. The sky was mostly clear and the moon gave enough light to show that the surrounding area was barren.

Anna yawned.

"Let me take over for a while. I got a good sleep. You've been up for hours."

The pod slowed to a gentle stop. Rubbing her eyes, Anna yawned again. "Okay. The flat ground is mesmerizing." She passed over her computer and leaned her seat back. Rolling onto her side, she smiled at him.

"What?" Luc set them off gently, increasing the speed until the back wheel protested, then eased off.

"Nothing."

Luc snickered. "Get some sleep, weirdo."

He drove through the night, only slowing down for the rare obstacle. He thought he saw a grove of trees in the distance, but it was another rock field. They weren't very big, but close enough together that he had to find a way around them. Eventually, the sun teased its arrival, illuminating a massive structure in the distance.

Luc straightened when he saw it and changed their course. His fatigue dissipated at the sight of anything on the surface of the mostly empty planet, and he increased their speed, even when the damaged rear wheel started to shudder.

When Telbak first came to the planet, they did

the normal cursory search for anything that could point to alien life—everything from liquid water that could hint at microbes to a lost civilization or signs of a previous extraterrestrial pit stop. It was standard practice on all colonies, though the only aliens humanity had discovered were the remains of single cell organisms, long dead.

Even then, the first settlers did their own search. Luc felt like it was a primal human driving force to explore. The second search confirmed the first. He knew that. But even still, the sight of the huge building in the middle of an otherwise desolate landscape sent chills up his arms.

As the shape became clear, he could tell it was a human structure—one of the gigantic terraforming complexes that circled the equator. He silently laughed at himself and cleared his throat, waking Anna.

She sat up and flinched when she saw it. "Oh, shit. I thought…"

"Me too." Luc covered a yawn.

The building looked like a huge pyramid with the top chopped off. Massive square pillars supported it on the four corners, lifting the façade up twenty feet before bending inward to meet at the top plateau. The interior was recessed between the pillars and on top were big smokestacks, half again as tall as the building itself. They spewed atmosphere and moisture into the sky. Heavy wet snow was piled up around it and out under the smoke that was carried away on artificial winds.

Anna rubbed her eyes. "You think this is the place?"

Luc slowed the vehicle as they approached. "We should go take a look."

Twenty-Eight
Manufactured Sky

Luc limped up a short flight of stairs. After he and Anna had smashed a window to get in, they split up, him heading down, her going up. He huffed as he pulled on the handrail and swung his leg up to the next step. "Shouldn't have chosen to go down."

He had walked the length of the facility, scanning for signals and checking vacant rooms. The machinery, creating atmosphere and struggling to maintain liveable temperatures on the planet, caused interference with his computer and the noise made hearing next to impossible. Still, he had thoroughly checked his half of the building and found nothing but the hissing pipes, dormant terminals, and layers of wet dust.

Cresting the top step, he hobbled to the front and out through the broken window. He saw her sitting in the pod and went to join her. They had set up the solar panel, but it wasn't getting much of the morning sun with the pyramidal structure casting such a large shadow. Pulling off his gloves, Luc rubbed his knee.

"I guess you didn't find anything either?"

Anna shook her head. "The place is huge, though. Maybe they're in some secret spot?"

Luc pressed his lips together. "I checked what systems I could without setting off any alarms. The power usage is typical, there are no hidden signals in the carrier waves." He shrugged. "I don't think they're here."

"How's the leg?" Anna furrowed her eyebrows.

"Sore. Not too bad. It gets stiff if I'm not using it." Taking out his computer, Luc scrolled through the maps and photos. "It seems like the right place."

"Uh huh." Anna bit her lip.

"We're in the area Dolly marked, but this structure isn't in the photos or the topographical scans."

"Maybe they're old? Done before it was built?"

Luc stretched. "It's possible, but they keep track of these complexes somehow. I doubt they send out crews regularly. It would make more sense that they use their satellites and the space station to keep tabs on them, and any other spots on the surface they find interesting."

Anna shrugged. "We could be in the wrong spot."

"I don't think so. All the other terraforming stations are accounted for." Luc gestured to the maps on his screen.

"Maybe Dolly's info was out of date?"

Sighing, Luc shut his eyes. "Could be any number of things, I guess. Shouldn't have thought it would be this easy to find the secret, hidden source of the broadcast."

"I wouldn't say it was easy." Anna shifted in her reclined seat to face him.

"No, but this final search, if it's here. It was always going to be a needle in a haystack." Patting her hand, Luc closed his computer. "If only we had some updated aerial photos. We don't even need anything that high up."

Anna sat up and dug her fingers into his arm.

"Ouch." Luc pulled away.

"The building."

"What?"

Anna pointed to the structure taking up the entire view in front of them. "This thing is really tall. Like, crazy tall."

Luc opened his eyes wider. "We can see the surrounding area from the top!" Stuffing his computer into his jacket, he opened the door. "Why didn't we think of it earlier?"

They ran back into the building, Luc falling behind.

Broadcast Wasteland

A droning hum originating somewhere in the lowest levels of the structure reverberated through every surface. Accompanying clunks, hisses, and sporadic high-pitched squeals added to the din.

They plodded down the painted concrete hallway, kicking up dust that mixed with the moisture in the air and came back down in wet clumps. Luc slipped going around a corner and Anna caught him.

"Thanks." He winced and limped more carefully to the elevator doors.

"No sweat." Anna smiled, her arm still wrapped around him.

A panel hung open, pried free earlier when they accessed the systems. Luc plugged his computer into a port and sent a command. The door opened with a ding and they went inside. Copying the action with the panel inside the car, Luc brought them to the top floor.

After the first few levels, the transparent side of the elevator faced the open interior of the complex and the angled windows. They both pressed their noses to the glass scanning the rocky surface for any indication of a broadcast source.

The elevator stopped abruptly, the momentum moving through them. They scrambled out the open door onto a narrow balcony open to the lobby many floors below. The angled windows were a few metres past the railing.

"This isn't the top." Anna looked left and right.

"I don't think so. There should be some stairs or a ladder for roof access."

"Which way?"

Luc shrugged and went left. At the end of the open corridor, they took another left. Behind a door, they found a metal staircase that continued up to the top.

Huffing, Luc grabbed the railing and took the first step. "Don't wait for me."

"I'm gonna." Anna poked him in the ribs.

"It's a long climb still."

She raised an eyebrow. "Start climbing, then."

They trudged up the steps to a locked door at the top. Luc tried bashing it open with his shoulder, but it didn't budge. He rubbed his arm as Anna took a closer look.

"I think we need something to pry the lock." She crossed her arms.

Luc scrunched his face and sighed. "There was a maintenance room on the main floor. I'll go see what I can find."

Anna snorted. "I'll go get it, peg leg. I don't want to spend all day up here waiting for you."

Luc sat on the top step and rubbed his knee until she came back.

Huffing and puffing, she handed him a screwdriver the length of his forearm. "Your…turn."

Broadcast Wasteland

Taking the screwdriver, he jammed the flat end into the space between the door and the frame and wrenched until the door swung open. Both out of breath, they went back out into the cold air.

The wind was fierce at the top of the building, whipping at their clothes and hair. Luc zipped up his jacket and hunched his shoulders. The flat top was wide and open, easily the same footprint as one of the skyscrapers back in the city. The stacks were set at opposite corners and were so large they nearly met in the middle. They were huge up close, like massive trees with billowing smoke as foliage. The heavy snow, forming as the atmosphere and moisture collided above them, fell in sheets, swirling in the ferocious wind.

Together, they walked to the closest edge and looked out over the ground far below. Even through the thick snow falling to the east, they could clearly see the featureless landscape. They tried another direction and saw a rocky ridge to the south with bare, dusty planes stretching out on the other side.

"There!" Anna pointed out a building to the north, one story high with a smaller second floor. The most notable feature was the large antenna. It wasn't nearly as tall as the ones near the city, but the framework rose well above the small building next to it.

"That's got it be it," she said.

Luc grimaced. "I mean. It seems like it."

Anna smacked him with the back of her hand. "Show a little excitement. It's probably the source of the broadcast." She started for the door, the wind catching her hair, making her ponytail swing. "What else could it be?"

Broadcast Wasteland

Twenty-Nine
The Broadcast

As they drove to the building, they found a dirt path between it and the complex that seemed to have been worn from years of people making the trip. Anna tapped her foot in the driver's seat. The back wheel was frantically shaking, almost in time with her.

"Luc, we did it." She was smiling.

"I hope so. We came a long way." Sitting upright and still, Luc stared out the windscreen. The snow fell behind them, but a few stray flakes dusted the pod. He watched the building get larger as they approached.

"What's wrong with you? I thought you'd be the excited one!"

"I don't know." Luc grimaced. "Something is bothering me."

"Ugh. Tri was right. You're not happy unless

things are going badly for you."

Luc crossed his arms and sighed. "Maybe, just… after everything, this seems really convenient."

"Don't give me that." Anna scowled at him. "This was hard. We came close to dying more than once."

"I know. I, uh." Luc shook his head. "Wouldn't they have found it? The Consortium? It's pretty close to the terraformer."

"It wasn't in the satellite photos, though. Maybe they're just good at hiding. You've gotten into the Consortium database and changed things before."

"Yeah, but nothing like this." Luc gestured to the building.

"We're almost there, just suck it up and get ready to be happy, for once."

She stopped the pod near the tower, a hundred metres or so from the building. Luc got out and checked the antenna. It was fenced off, but a gate was open. He connected his computer and checked the outgoing transmissions.

"This seems to be it. Or at least a relay station." He unplugged and put his computer away.

"See. What did I tell you?" Anna went around to the front of the building. "We made—"

Luc followed, limping. "What was that?" He used the wall for support, the rough brick felt sharp in the cold. "Anna?"

As he rounded the corner he spotted a Consortium Operative. The person was in a synth leather suit, black with red stripes, and wore a helmet with an opaque mask. They held Anna in a tight grip.

Luc froze, but a voice to his right drew his attention. "Hello, Luc. It took you long enough to get here."

He nearly fell to his knees, all the fight knocked out of him. Managing to take another step, he saw another Operative and several soldiers. He didn't bother counting them. Even one would have been enough.

Dmitri moved next to his sister. He was smiling, practically manically. "I got you. I planned this whole thing and not only did you walk right into my trap, but you managed to flush out people who I've been trying to corner for months now."

Breathing in deeply, Dmitri moved closer to Luc. "I'd been watching Tri, but she had a benefactor keeping her from me. Thanks to you, I was able to catch her red-handed and there was nothing the manager could do. As for Dolly and Shadow, everyone knew what they were up to, but they had off world contacts and advanced systems protecting them, until you showed up." Dmitri leaned in. "I got both of them and I got the Rancore Siblings, and that filthy diner cook, those loser kids who look up to you, and everyone who even had a conversation with you for the last year."

Laughing, Dmitri walked past Luc and faced the tower. "My first mission was to find this place. I've been the one running things for a while now, sending out the broadcast. I got you to come all the way out here just to walk into my trap." He turned back to Luc. "I won."

"What, do you want me to say it?" Luc swallowed. "You won. You beat me."

"Oh, I don't care about that. I knew I would." Dmitri's smile disappeared. He sneered and got in Luc's face. "I'm upset. I'm angry. I told you to keep my sister out of it, and you not only dragged her out here, you put her in danger."

"Dmitri!" Anna struggled in the Operative's grip. "I'm the one who convinced—"

"Keep your mouth shut!" Spittle flew from Dmitri. "I'll deal with you later." Breathing deeply, he calmed down. "Right now, I have to decide what to do with Luc."

"Not going to send me to the mines?" Luc clenched his jaw.

"No. You burned that bridge a long time ago. My choices are to take you in and kill you later, or just do it now and save myself the hassle."

Luc scrunched up his face. He counted to ten, cleared his throat, and counted back down to one. Sighing, he looked back at Dmitri. "You've always been an asshole. Even when we were kids. I may not have been an angel, but I was never a little creep. You caught me, tricked me, but you'll never be better than me."

"Luc. Don't." Anna fought again, but the Operative kept her in place as if it were as easy as standing still.

"Thanks for making my choice for me." Dmitri held out a hand and one of the soldiers gave him a gun.

A shadow crept over them followed by others, rolling past. One stayed in place overhead and grew in all directions.

Luc looked up and saw ships. Dozens, a hundred, maybe more. Most were small, but there were two that hung in place, larger than any ships Luc had ever seen—easily twice the size of the colony ship. They descended so quickly it was like they were falling. As the first of them approached, thrusters shot out from underneath, halting their plummeting dive.

A few shuttles landed in the barren space between the building and the distant terraforming complex, but the one hovering overhead didn't move. Ropes rolled out, dropping to the ground, and soldiers in Telbak blue slid down them, firing on the Consortium troops.

The Operative holding Anna released his grip

and started to return fire, prompting his comrades to join in.

Anna ran to Luc and caught him as his legs gave out. They fell, holding each other while the firefight broke out around them. More Telbak soldiers joined the fray, running in from every direction. The Consortium was wiped out in a minute. Some of the guards gave up, kneeling with their hands in the air—others were dead, their bodies laying in heaps on the cold ground. Dmitri stood with the gun in his still outstretched hand. He watched the battle passively, not moving.

As the fighting stopped, two Telbak Operatives came towards Luc and Anna while the soldiers dealt with those who had surrendered.

A man in a brown jacket went up to Dmitri and took away his gun. "Stand down. We got you outnumbered and the rest of your squad already gave up."

"Or they're dead." A woman stopped next to him, adding a hop to the action. She wore a blue and black coat with a huge Telbak symbol wrapping around the back. Her pink hair was pulled up into a Mohawk that bobbed along with her movement. "We got you gooood."

She seemed to notice Anna and Luc and skipped over to them. "Got something over here, Reg." Squatting down next to them, she held out her hand.

"Hey there. I'm Teal, that grump behind me is Reggie. We're here to take back this colony. Be you friend or foe?"

Anna shook her head. "We're hackers. That's my brother. He lured us out here and was going to kill Luc."

Teal stood. "That's not very nice. We're going to put him in custody. I assume you're okay with that?"

Nodding, Anna helped Luc stand.

"Something wrong with your legs?" Teal pointed at Luc.

Reggie let one of the soldiers in blue take Dmitri to the other Consortium personnel who were being put into cuffs and led to one of the ships.

"Give them a break, Teal. They've clearly been through a lot," he said.

"I know, I'm just really, really excited." A smile broke out on Teal's face. "This is my first mission as an Operative."

Luc coughed. "You're taking back the city?"

Reggie nodded. "The whole planet. This is just one of our strike teams. We have more landing at every complex. Once we're in place, we'll take the city."

"There are thousands of innocent people there!" Anna said.

Teal grabbed her shoulder. "We know. Don't worry. We're going to save them all. We already took out the space station and most of their defences. We've been controlling their satellites for weeks."

Luc smiled. "The network." He looked to Reggie. "What does that mean for us?"

Reggie furrowed his eyebrows. "We're setting this building up as a field base. You can stay here for now. We'll have someone take a look at your injuries. Maybe you can even help us. We don't have a lot of specific information on the city or what the Consortium has been doing here. After that?" He shrugged. "You'll be Telbak citizens. You can do whatever you want."

Luc felt tears well up in his eyes. He smiled and faced Anna. She was crying and let out a weak laugh.

He stared into her eyes and the bedlam around them faded away. He put his hand on the small of her back, but before he could lean in, she kissed him.

"Sorry. I've been waiting for too long."

He laughed. "It's okay. I'm sorry for making you wait."

COMING SOON
BREAK/ INTERRUPT

Acknowledgements

This book, more than any others I've written, left me staring at the forest and missing the trees. It's thanks to the patience and effort of a number of wonderful people that I was able to release it at all. After such a great feeling with The Neon Heart, this new book seemed so different. I couldn't tell if that was different good or if I had gone completely off the rails. I'm happy with how it turned out and with the growth of my writing chops over the course of writing and editing it.

As always, a huge thanks has to go to Christian Laforet. When I was most doubtful, he was brave enough to read a very rough second draft of this book and reassure me that there was something worth salvaging. He also confirmed my suspicions that some of it had to go. It's been a long journey, but his help has made it at lot easier.

My parents have never stopped looking out for me, and I don't know where I would be without that love and support. It's a lot of work writing these books, publishing them, and releasing them to a world that owes me nothing. Working a part time job in order to focus on writing is another step farther. Knowing that they have my back makes it possible. I can never thank them enough.

My brother Jake takes things even more to heart and even lets me live at his house. I couldn't manage without that kindness. He is a constant source of encouragement and inspiration and I'm forever in awe of his talent.

I have to give credit to the writers group Write On Windsor for helping me develop the tools to write and publish a book. They are a constant resource that I share with as many hopeful authors as I can.

My personal writing friends are a lifeline on which I depend often. Whether it's getting together at a coffee shop to work, asking random questions at odd hours, or just talking about what we're all working on, they help keep me going when I struggle.

The amazing cover was done by the talented and enthusiastic Glen Hawkes. In a single meeting, he sketched out the idea on a napkin and had the final version done in a week. He was open to tweaking things and happy for the feedback. We even worked on one of his projects when it was done. I'm ecstatic to have such a fantastic face on the cover of this book. I hope he's up for the next one.

The people who did beta reads and reviews for this book deserve more than I can give them. If there are any mistakes in the text, it's completely my fault despite their best efforts.

Christian Laforet, Brittni Brinn, Elly Blake, Justin Cantelo, James Martin, Melissa Schnarr-Rice, Sephorah Pohjola, Lori Lorimer, Jake Van Dongen, and Bob and Deborah Van Dongen all took the time to try and make this book readable. I thank them all for their hard work.

Ben Van Dongen was born in Windsor Ontario. He likes to think that if he tried harder he could have been an Astronaut, but he is happier writing science fiction anyway. He wrote the Synthetic Albatross Novella Series, co-authored the books No Light Tomorrow and All These Crooked Streets, and is one half of the founding team of Adventure Worlds Press. You can read more crazy notions on his website. **BenVanDongen.com**

Photo by Khoa Nguyen

AdventureWorldsPress.com

More Books by the Author

The Synthetic Albatross Series

The Earth Books
The Thinking Machine
The Neon Heart
Break/Interrupt

The Offworld Books
Broadcast Wasteland

Anthologies
No Light Tomorrow
All These Crooked Streets